CHUBBY SEASONS

FALL

Chapter 1

---◄◆◆►---

We had just won our 3rd State Championship in football and I was waiting on the field for my boyfriend, Dylan. "BABE we won." Dylan was holding me in his arms so elated from the win. He nearly lifted me off the ground. "After school we are gonna go to the movies with the crew. Then, I am gonna take you out to the best restaurant in town baby." Then he leaned in for a kiss on the cheek. I loved Dylan so much.

"Hey! Hey!" My mom caught me daydreaming about another TV show that I wished were reality. "Monica, can you believe it, your first day of high school." Summer had just ended and as I rode in my mom's 1991 White Acclaim the radio was blasting an old tape of Salt N Pepa's *Shoop*. My mom loved that song. She played that song so much I could rap it to the letter. I had my seat-belt on and my knees were shaking. I glanced over and my mom was fixing her makeup in the mirror. My mom was considered in her day a stone-cold fox. She was a perfect 5'5 and slim in all the right places. A former captain of the cheerleaders. Oh, she was also prom queen. Perfect dark brown eyes, bouncy shoulder-length dark brown hair. She also always wore the best fashions. Every time I went somewhere it's like everybody wanted to know where Veronica Clark was. It was like I was invisible. A definite show-stopper. Most folks thought we were sisters instead of mother daughter. She paused from putting on her makeup and said, "Okay, Woo, you ready?" Woo is a nickname my mom gave me short for Whoopie, which I never figured out her rationale for calling me that name, but it stuck like glue. I was thinking, *Am I ready for this?* After binge watching Beverly Hills 90210 and watching Moesha, I thought I was mentally prepared for the experience of a lifetime. Would I be popular and date a million boys? Or would I be a lame and be confined to a lunch table full of burn-outs reeking of marijuana and no dreams? Or just a girl that didn't exist? High school, the place that makes or breaks you. The place that would determine if you went to college. Lastly, it was a place where you would make lifelong friends. I remember that day. I wore a yellow and blue pleated skirt that came about mid-thigh. I had black flats for shoes and a white-collar shirt with black circle buttons going down the front. My hair was perfectly braided in single dark brown braids. It would take 6 hours to get them done but it was worth the time. I was dressed just like Moesha and fly, so I thought. The year was 1996 and I was a freshman at Jeffersonville High School. Last school year I was in middle school. I was… let's say… not the most popular. I had no boyfriends and barely friends. I never understood why at first. Then I figured maybe it's because I was 6'0" tall in the 8th grade with a belly that overlapped my pants a little. I also had a butt that could flag down traffic and a set of thighs that was in need of a thigh master. I had a caramel latte complexion with almond shaped eyes and skin like smooth butter (according to my family). My mom even made me get a jheri curl my 6th grade year. I thought it was cool until my classmates reminded me the style was better left in the 80s. My fashion choices were boarding between horrible and a walking disaster. I pretty much just did my schoolwork and watched TV. I would escape into the popularity of the TV characters. Brenda Walsh and Moesha Mitchell. It was my only way to escape the horrors of being the joke of every conversation. By the way my name is Monica Johnson... But in middle school it was Mon or Big Mon. Not the greatest nickname when you're trying to get your first kiss. Now, I am a freshman in a new school district. Nobody knows me here. My mom and I moved over here because the community of Jeffersonville was a step up for us economically. Previously, we stayed about 45 minutes away in Jackson, IN. Jackson was actually really diverse. It had every race known to the imagination and was lower-middle class. Most people worked in the steel mills that were left, K-mart, or a small business. We had a little apartment that was minutes away from my old school. Our spot had 1 bedroom for my mom, and I slept on the let-out couch. My mom worked at this little law firm in the mail room while going to college part-time. We didn't have a lot, but she always made it work. At the end of spring, she got a promotion to legal secretary, but it would have to be in Jeffersonville. It was a big deal because we could afford a bigger place and I could start over. In fact, when she told me about it, she was shocked that I was so excited to move. I nearly broke my foot jumping up off the let-out couch when she told me we were moving. We found a nice 2-bedroom apartment and I finally had my own room. A friend of hers lived there and knew an apartment had opened up. Apparently, some couple moved to Los Angeles to help take care of a sick aunt. The apartment had a lot of young doctors and young couples just starting out their lives. The most thrilling was I didn't have to worry about random people sitting on my bed when we had company. I always had to wait until everyone left when mommy had company just so I could go to bed. I had grown to like mommy friends. They were so nice to me. Although we had so much fun together, I always wished I had friends to hang with and talk about my crushes to clothing choices. Plus, mom had to work a lot so it was hard to find our girl time. Mom always knew when I needed it. We would make pallets on the floor and eat Broncos pizza after rough days at school. My mom introduced me to all the classic movies that gave me hope of finding love one day. I really hoped this new job gave us more time together, especially with living in a new town. We moved in June and that gave me time to look around the town before starting high school. From what I could see Jeffersonville was an upper middle-class town where you would get a snarky look if there were no Christmas lights on your home during the holiday season. These people cared about their lawns so much if you walked across the grass the sprinklers would soak you. I came home from the local food spot, Uno's, drenched from accidentally walking through someone's lawn. Apparently, the dirty look I gave them didn't get them to turn off the sprinklers. The summer flew by and I spent most of it walking around and writing in my journal. Writing let me slip away into a land of love and peace. It didn't remind me of the bullying I endured daily from people that for some reason got a kick out of making me feel bad. I glanced at my mother as I got ready for a new start. I walked up the steps thinking, *Big Mon is gone. Hello, Monica, your new life starts NOW!!!*

Chapter 2

"Hey, move out the way, freshman." Those are the words I heard walking down the hallway to my first class. At least it wasn't "Hey, fat butt," which is what I am used to hearing. I was literally rubbing shoulders with my fellow classmates. I had my class schedule glued to my hands, afraid to look up and be remembered as I was in middle school. I finally heard this loud voice say, "Dang girl, you lost." I looked up really quickly, and after bumping my head into her perfectly ironed out light brown hair, "Girl, you play too much." I thought, *wow, jess was one of the few people I knew in middle school that was nice to me.* She said, "Who you got for first hour?"

I said, "Somebody named Mrs. Roberts." It was English 1, our first high school class. That friend was Jessica, or Jess as folks knew her. Jess was about 5'7 and had a lean model figure. She was almond complexioned with distinctively long legs. I vaguely remembered that in middle school her mom and dad were well off, but she never brought her mom around much except for rides. She had hazel brown eyes and long hair always covering one eye like Aaliyah, the singer. She went out of the district because of the cheer squad in Jackson. I still didn't understand why her parents drove so far just for cheer. After I saw all the trophies in the hallway, I knew the middle school team was awesome. They traveled nearly every weekend in the spring and won so many trophies. However, at Jeffersonville High School, this team had won State Championships every year for the last 10 years. I secretly prayed, even though I was a new kid, that she would be here. I wanted a fresh start. It's always good to see peeps that are cool. Jess always spoke to me and never once made fun of my looks. We walked into the class and I started to panic. I felt my heart beat a million times a second. There were about 13 boys in the class and 11 girls. All dressed in the late 90s fashion. Fresh Jordans everywhere, the boys wore a mix of Mecca and oversized Fubu shirts. Also wearing jeans that would expose random parts of their boxer shorts due to sagging (A trend I never quite understood). The girls would wear colorful Skechers with random Tommy Hilfiger crop tops and baggy jeans. Hey, it was '96 and fashion had no bounds. My outfit was actually fashion appropriate. My mom worked hard to get me the perfect outfit to start school in and I was proud. Jess and I were sitting in the middle of the class. I had my fluffy pink pen thinking I was Alicia Silverstone in *Clueless* and my purple notebook ready to take notes. Looking around the classroom, I noticed Jess was passing a note to a boy behind us. She didn't look too happy. Even I could smell the boy's breath from across the class. I was rapidly taking notes, partly to avoid looking dumb on the first day, then the bell rang. Feeling relieved, I let out a big deep breath. I had made it through my first class of high school.

My next class was algebra and then P.E, which sucked because we had swimming and your hair would be destroyed before the day got started. That's another reason I was glad to have my braids. So far, my first day was going off without a hitch. Until I reached the cafeteria. I began to freak out about where I would sit. Would Jess be there?

Pausing, I looked around feeling dizzy from scanning the tables. Then I saw it …..... *Oh noo, the burnnnnn out table!* That table was drawing me to it like it needed me. This is where I would fit in. The place for 6'0" chubby girls with hardly any friends. The place where people go to escape reality. It had its perks due to you having some friendships and maybe getting invited to a sleepover to discuss boys you never could date. It was better than nothing. In addition, the guys at the table didn't smell too bad if you liked onions. I took a big gulp and shook my head back. My long braids flew to the back. I was on my way to burnout land when I heard Jess say, "Hey, Mon, over here." She was waving me over frantically as if she secretly knew my high school career would depend on where I would sit in the cafeteria. I mean, in every high school movie I saw the cafeteria was the place to make you cool or yesterday's news. I walked over to the table and I had a flashback to 6th grade. I was dressed in a Karl Kani short set with a fresh Jheri curl from the beauty shop. Standing there, I looked around and the only seat was next to the security guard in the school. I was so tall half the kids thought I was staff. "Mon…Mon." Jess was calling me over…It was the call of service; 4 years of popular duty avoided a lifetime of pain. When I blinked my eyes, I began walking, Jess was enjoying some French fries while talking. I could see her large hoop earrings dangling as her head moved like it was some serious gossip at the table. My head was thinking, *is my skirt too short or should I have worn my Kenneth Cole shoes my grandmother bought me?* I mean, this school was sort of in the rich part of town. Most of the kids had cars and 2 parent homes. I thought, *Screw this! I am going over there.* As I sat down, there were 2 other girls sitting at the table. Everyone had purses or mini backpacks. And me...I had this huge blue backpack like a 5th grader. Oh well, I would correct that later shopping with mom if she had the money. The first girl was a short chocolate girl with brown hair. She had a gymnast build and a short haircut like Halle Berry and big pearly white teeth. Only her name was Rochelle, Shelly for short. Shelly had just come to Jeffersonville from South Carolina and she had a really thick accent. She was the sweet one of the crew. At times, she struggled academically due to her lack of study skills. She had 3 younger siblings that took up her time. She was always fussing about those brats every day. Next, was a girl with long light brown curly hair. She was light skinned with defined cheekbones. She reminded me of Lisa Turtle from *Saved by The Bell* only fairer, her name was Ashley. She certainly had the fashion, as she wore a yellow Gap crop top with a long flower printed skirt with white Skechers. Ashley came from a decent family and she had an older brother that was a senior. I remember her saying how much she hated her older brother because he always had girls over at their house. The only thing that bothered me about Ashley is she talked super-fast. I mean super-duper fast. Your eyes would go cross just listening to her. I did admire how close she was to her mom if you could catch the words as she talked about their relationship. Sitting there, the questions flew at me like 90 miles per hour fast balls. "Do you have a boyfriend?" "What movies do you like?" "Do you have a car?" "Do you have the new Skechers?" Unfortunately, most of these questions were a big, FAT NO. The closest thing I had to a boyfriend was someone from church camp who only kissed me to see if he was gay. My lips suffered the most damage though, due to homeboy's metal gear mouth. The rest of the questions required some form of spending money, which my mother barely had.

My mom was a single mother. Unlike 90 percent of the kids at the school, my mom had divorced. She never told me why dad wasn't around, I just knew I never had one. Whenever the thought crossed my mind and I asked about him, she would always say, "Woo (a family nickname), I know you will meet him one day. Trust me it's safer for you to not know him right now." I just pretended that my dad was royalty and, for my protection, he didn't come around. My mom worked at a law firm now, and although we weren't *poor* poor, we sure didn't have money to shop every weekend, but she tried her best. At the table, I spoke like I had some knowledge of today's popular culture. From Backstreet Boys to Boys 2 Men, and Jess made me feel comfortable. Then it dawned on me. I was at the popular table. It felt as though a spotlight was shining on the table from Star Search only I was the one being scored.

Even as freshmen these girls were gorgeous by any standard. I wasn't used to these pretty girls talking to me and actually liking my opinion. But as soon as I got comfortable, a boy walked over. He was about 6'3" full of muscles and wearing a red Bulls basketball jersey with a white t-shirt underneath and baggy jeans. His name was Jason. He literally spoke to all the girls at the table except me but that was to be expected; I was used to being ignored by guys. As the lunch hour wound down, I decided the following: I was lucky to be with a group of pretty girls. My former popular mom would be happy that I had a fun crew. Over the next few weeks, we shared and talked about everything. I went over to their homes and so many shopping adventures. We got close and I was happy but I would have to accept my role as the chubby girl with pretty friends.

Chapter 3

―――――◆―◆―◆―――――

A hhh…Assembly time! Every once and a while we would meet in this large auditorium to congratulate random scholarly achievements. You could feel proud for actually studying. However, this particular assembly was to recognize the State Champion Football Team and to give them their rings. Last year, in a story book win, our Jeffersonville High Cougars won the game on a field goal. I remember everyone in the neighborhood was talking about it all the way in Jackson. The town of Jeffersonville had come alive. With Jeffersonville, IN being a sports town, all you could see was blue and gold around the entire city. My mom still remembers cheering against Jeffersonville for regional and state championships in the 70s. I would sit around and listen to her talk to her friends about the good ol days when cheer hadn't become so proper. As the auditorium erupted with cheers for sophomore Jason Whitmore, the football team's MVP, I began to wonder if I would ever be congratulated for such an achievement in sports. Or even more, would I be able to date someone like that? I mean in my middle school body…NEVER. But I had some positive features, at least, that's what my grandmother says. Underneath my braids was thick long hair that I hated to comb because it stayed tangled for some reason. And my legs, my aunt says, would run on for days. But, for some reason, people just saw the chubby girl…

I whispered to Shelly, "How long do you think this assembly will last?" Shelly said in an annoyed voice, "I hope not too much longer, because I want to practice before they start cheer team tryouts this afternoon." After the assembly, all of us girls were walking in the freshman hallway. Jess asked, "Does everyone have their cheers ready?" Everyone replied excitedly, yep sure do. Jess says, "Ok, because you know Coach Minnie does *not* play." At exactly 3:45, I was surrounded by my crew of Shelly, Jess, and Ashley wearing black shorts and white tank tops. As we sat on the Jefferson High Cougar mascot at center court, I noticed everyone either looked really confident or about to puke. Then, Coach Minnie appeared. It was like slow motion watching her walk in the gym. This woman appeared to have not let go of the 80s. She had thick, frizzy hair with neon green thunderbolt earrings along with bright red lipstick to boot. She asked us all to stand up and introduce ourselves. One by one, everybody spoke up. However, when it was my turn, I just couldn't seem to remember a thing. Oh nooo. My thoughts were everywhere. How would my mom answer these girls? Then I simply looked up and said in a rather loud voice, "Hi, everyone, my name is Monica Johnson and I am a freshman!" You could hear my voice bounce all over the gym walls. Now came the time to show my stuff. Coach Minnie asked us to spread out on the floor and gave us 5 minutes to practice. I quickly ran over to a corner in the gym, right next to the bleachers. You see, the night before my mom and I had practiced. We rehearsed cheers well into the night. My mom wouldn't let me go to sleep until I knew the infamous Paul Revere Cheer. She and her friends had won the State Cheer title with this cheer:

Now listen my children and you shall HEAR

About the midnight ride of Paul Revere

Going up the Alley

And Down the Street

Saying Tornadoes Tornadoes

Can't be beat

Singing, AHH OHHH OHHH

"Monica Johnson," someone was loudly yelling at me to come and start my cheer. In front of the gym was a bright yellow table with 4 people sitting in black folding chairs. Of course, Coach Minnie was there but also 3 seniors that were captains of the cheer squad. I walked up to the table and backed up about 8 feet. I started to shout my cheer. Shouted it so loud my throat squeaked.

"Now listen my children and you shall HEAR

About the midnight ride of Paul Revere

Going up the Alley

And Down the Street

Saying Cougars Cougars

Can't be beat

Singing, AHH OHHH OHHH"

After the cheer, I just stood there. Coach Minnie looked happy, but the other captains had a look of confusion. Their eyebrows reached nearly the top of their foreheads. Hey, but I felt good about my cheer.

"Next," they said in a loud military voice, "Cartwheel, please." I did my cartwheel with perfection.

Then the captains said in unison, "Back handspring."

I said confused, "A what?" They started laughing and said, "A back handspring, ya know?" But I didn't know, my mom hadn't prepared me for this. All she taught me was a cheer, a cartwheel, and a split. Needless to say, I sure couldn't do a back handspring. So, I just did 2 cartwheels to compensate for the back handspring. After my turn, I went to the locker room and sat with my towel around my neck, looking towards the ceiling, thinking it may not be so bad. After all, maybe they just wanted to see me do a back handspring for extra points. Shelly interrupted my thoughts and asked, "Do you think you made it?"

I said confidently, "Sure girl, how about you?"

Shelly looked unsure and said, "My back handspring landing was kind of wobbly, but I think my basket toss was FIRE!" I scratched my head thinking, what in the world is a basket toss. Jess came running over and excitedly said, "Yo they are announcing the squad during Friday assembly. So, make sure y'all look good for when they call our names." I jumped up from the bench and thought of Jason getting all of those accolades. I would be next, and my popularity would for sure skyrocket.

The bell rang and all the students piled into the auditorium Friday morning. First, we all stood and stated the Pledge of Allegiance. This girl named Jackee, a junior, started to sing our school song. Nobody told me Jackee sounded like a cat holding on to the bark of a tree. I turned my head to the right tensely to get the screeching sound out of my ear. Jess and I sat next to each other since we had English class 1st period. I hadn't been more excited for today. I mean sure I didn't know any of that stuff, but I was a freshman, and I probably wasn't the only one that couldn't do flipping stuff. Anyway, Jackee was still butchering the school song. I whispered to Jess, "Hey I am gonna run to the restroom."

Jess whispered back, "You're gonna miss the list."

I replied, "No, I won't, I just need to use the bathroom." Jess, not being the one for excuses, gave me a stern look and said, "Girl, hurry up." I bent down and quietly said, "Excuse me" as I was walking through the aisle in the auditorium. Once I got to the bathroom, I checked my outfit. My braids were down, and I wore a blue jean hat with a purple flower like from *Blossom* the TV show. My body shirt was purple and snapped at the bottom. I wore wide leg blue jean pants to match my hat. My mom helped me pick out my outfit the night before. I stood in front of the mirror and did a quick turn. I put both hands on my hips while looking in the mirror and thought, *Mon, this is it. Cheer Team, here we go!* Lucky for me, Jackee had ad libbed so much to the school song that she was just finishing up when I sat back down. After the crowd awoke from Jackee's singing, the atmosphere changed as soon as Coach Minnie walked out. All the girls' faces looked like this list was going to be the celebrities of our school. The boys just looked overheated and wanted to snag a cheerleader. But me, I was happy either way. I would have a date or be considered a celeb. Coach Minnie grabbed the microphone and started to read slowly. I never noticed but Coach Minnie had a slight lisp when she read. Jess, Shelly, and Ashley's names were called first. Then 5 other names. Oh nooo. There are only 2 spots left. My feet started to tap…Then I heard Kelly James, and lastly Farrah Wilds. As I started to stand and leave the assembly, Jess pulled my arm to try and talk to me. But I left, I didn't want to talk yet. I began to think maybe I should have gone to Jess's house and practiced with the other girls instead of listening to my mom's old 1979 cheer routines. Oh well, I had become used to disappointment. Watching TV in the afternoons and on weekends wouldn't be so bad. That had been my life anyway. I saw Coach Minnie after assembly down the hall. I mean, who could miss that bright blue eye-shadow and high teased hair. She was waving at me to come toward her. I suddenly got excited. Had there been a mistake? Did one of the girls quit already? I walked down the hall like no one was there, just Coach Minnie and me. I stood in front of her waiting for the news, as a few students were being nosy wanting to hear our conversation. Coach Minnie, scratching her forehead, looked at me and said, "Hey, Johnson, I loved your cheer by the way." As she patted her teased hair, she told me, "You know, it reminded me about back in my day." Coach Minnie's lisp was even more prevalent.

I said, "Thank you Coach Minnie."

She said, "Look, although you didn't make the team. You can still be the Team Manager."

I quickly said, nearly cutting her off, "MANAGER?" We began to walk slowly, she said, "Yes, you can help wash uniforms and carry bags, you know that stuff. It will also give you a chance to train and sharpen your skills." I started to blink with a fury. I took off my hat and scratched the crown of my head.

"Johnson!" Coach Minnie yelled.

I answered, "Yes, coach."

"In or out?" Coach Minnie said. I put on my hat, stood up nice and tall and said, "Sure, when is practice?"

As I walked home that evening I began to cry. I gripped my bookbag straps tightly and just let the tears flow. I kept thinking that high school would be different, and I wouldn't be just the chubby girl who got looked over. All of the insults came rushing back to my head. Fat, giant, and most of all, ugly. Those were all the words I heard in middle school. Hearing them was part of my normal day. So much so that if I didn't hear them, I thought something was wrong. When I got home, I couldn't even look at my mom, who came home earlier than expected.

She asked, "So, how did it go?" I just stood and looked at her with a sadness in my eyes. She touched my chin and noticed that my eyes were puffy and red from crying. I said nothing. My mother knew that I had no words. She also knew I didn't make the team. But, I would get it over it soon. All I needed was a standard hug and a pep talk and life would go on. I was used to disappointment and had mastered how to move on.

Ironically, I settled into the role of team manager for the Jefferson High-school Cheer Squad quite well. I got to wear a blue polo shirt with a little J in cursive along with gold jogger pants for my uniform. I was becoming a better cheerleader since I would fill in for girls often. Every Friday during football season was Spirit Day. Every team would wear their team uniforms to show school spirit. This included all team managers as well. Although I wasn't a cheerleader, I was still a part of something, which was more than some could say. These Fridays were special. It was also a time where all the girls could wear their boyfriend's jerseys or paint their faces with their boyfriend's jersey number. Jess had started dating Michael Sanders at this point. But we all called him Mike. He played wide receiver for the team and was a junior. Mike was about 5'10" and slender. He had an athletic build, which he didn't mind showing any chance he got. His skin was smooth chocolate along with dark brown eyes. He wore his hair with a low-cut fade with a little dash line in the front. Shelly and Ashley had been dating as well but nothing serious. As I walked down the freshman hall, Jess and Mike were walking with me, Shelly, and Ashley. The girls were in their cheer uniforms and Mike wore his team jersey. Mike had placed his arm around Jess just to remind everyone that she was taken. I walked along carrying my English and Algebra books, feeling good. Hey, I was in the cool crowd, it couldn't get much better. Later, that evening the whole cheer squad met up for the game at the football field gate. It was chilly for a September night at 53 degrees, so the cheer squad wore their gold joggers. I sat in the stands next to Coach Minnie to pass out water as needed.

Chapter 4

O uch!" I stood up quickly and grimaced. Our quarterback had just taken a nasty hit to his ribs and it was only the second quarter of the game. I sat back down on the bleachers next to Coach Minnie who was in shock. There was a mix of cries and open mouths as Randy was laid out on the field. The cheerleaders were on the track in front of me, all taking a knee. Some people were even praying. I just kept my head down in my lap, hoping for Randy to get up. Then I looked over and the football team had broken their huddle. Randy was up but limping off the field. Everyone stood up and clapped as Randy left for the locker rooms. Next up would be Jason, the team's backup quarterback. You would think he was an NFL player the way the crowd responded to him. We ended up winning the game 20-14 due to Jason throwing for over 200 yards and 2 touchdowns. The cheerleaders all crowded him after the game, even my girls. I just sat in the bleachers with Coach Minnie and talked with her about the schedule for next week's practice.

She said, "I want you to remind all the girls about the new schedule Sunday evening."

I responded, "Yes, ma'am, I am gonna call them all Sunday night." Coach Minnie was determined they practice more next week. Homecoming was next month, and she wanted their field routine to be clean and tight. I yelled to Jess, "Hey, Jess, wait up, can I get a ride with you?"

Jess said, "Yea, girl, come on. My mom is already in the parking lot." I rushed and got all of the poms and equipment put away so I could meet Jess at her parent's car. The parking lot was packed. Anybody who mattered were all standing outside their cars discussing the after-party. You could hear Ginuwine's "Pony" bumping in the lot where the cheer team was standing. I ran out to the lot and stood near the freshman cheerleaders. I said to Shelly and Ashley, "Where is Jess?"

Ashley replied, "Girl, she's over there talking to Mike." I rolled my eyes. It's not that I didn't like Mike, it's just that I hadn't heard good things about him and didn't want Jess to get hurt. Finally, I gathered the courage and went over and whispered to Jess, "Hey, girl, your mom is waiting, we better roll." Jess's eyes got really big.

She then said, "Oh crap, let's go!" Mike stepped in between us and said, "Hey, we are gonna roll over to Jason's to celebrate, you wanna go?"

Jess said flirtatiously, "Maybe later I gotta check with my mom."

Mike said, "Ok well hit my pager if you can get out the crib." As we walked to the car, I was carrying my gym bag on my shoulder. For not being a cheerleader, I was exhausted.

Jess then asked, "You think my mom would let me go?"

I said, "I don't know Jess, your mom is kind of ...you know."

Jess said, "Kind of what?"

I said, "Um...strict." I remembered a night at Jess's house when I spent the night. Jess's house was amazing. It was a large 4-bedroom brick home with a pool in the backyard. Also, her basement was da bomb. It had a pool table with these bar stools around the gray walls. The floor model TV would sit across from the wood burning fireplace. Jess's mom was a housewife, and her dad was a doctor. The first week of school, her mom was really upset about Jessica not getting an A on a science project. Jess had gotten a B, but her mom wouldn't let her go out for 2 weeks because of that B. Now, walking to the car with Jess, I knew that we had another paper due Monday. Her mom, being the strict one, was not going to allow her out for a party.

As we got to the car I said, "Hey just ask her, and then say we are studying together Saturday afternoon." That's what she did, and her mom allowed her to go. I guess my street cred with parents was good. I mean I was just the chubby friend and team manager. What trouble could she get in with me?

Chapter 5

———◆—◆—◆———

After Jess dropped me off at home, I began to think, *what did I just get myself into? A party? What do you even wear? How would I do my hair?* I walked through the door and yelled, "Mom, are you home?"

She replied, "Yes, I am in my room folding laundry." My mom's room was pretty simple. It had horizontal white blinds in the windows with a black entertainment stand with all types of movies you could ever want. Her bed was queen-sized with a gold and black comforter set. I loved watching *Pretty Woman* and *Coming to America* so much. I think I may have broken the VHS tape. Her closet was not too large, but it managed to fit hundreds of outfits from every decade she lived. My mom was a firm believer in not throwing away clothes because she always would say, you never know when you'll need an outfit. I personally needed an outfit to wear to this party. All I had were cheer jogging suits, a couple of pairs of baggy jeans, and some Fubu t-shirts. I mostly was a jean and t-shirt kind of girl. My mom never really took me shopping for the latest fashions, but she certainly shopped. I remember sitting in the clothing store, Gantos, for hours while my mom tried on every outfit in the store. The frustrating part is she probably didn't want to buy anything and just wanted to feel special.

Sitting on her queen-sized bed, I asked "Mom can you help me find something to wear to this party."

She said with eagerness, "What party?"

I said, "The football team is having a party and Jess, the girls, and I were invited." Secretly I was thinking if I could only fit in my mom's clothes, I wouldn't have this issue. After my mom ironed out the basics of the whos and wheres of the party, we began to look for anything that may look decent in my teeny-tiny closet. I couldn't believe this crap. I had nothing. Nothing that even remotely that looked comparable to what the girls in high school wore daily. After 30 minutes, I sat on my twin-sized bed feeling defeated. I began to think maybe I shouldn't go and just stay home and watch *Pretty Woman* or *Coming to America*. I mean, it wasn't like Jason wanted me to go anyway, I was just the tag along. Just when I was about to get off the bed and leave the room, my mom started to scream. I turned around rather quickly as I thought something was wrong.

While catching her breath, she said, "This is it. This is what you're going to wear." I flopped back down on the bed to get a closer look. My mom managed to find an old dress that she had bought me to wear to my cousin's wedding over the summer. I had completely forgotten about it since the weather had changed. It was a long floral printed red dress with thin spaghetti straps. My mom had also found a gray fitted shirt to wear underneath it since it was cooler and September. I also had my shoes from the wedding: a pair of open toed black sandals with a kitten heel. I was 6'0 and didn't want to tower over anyone. I finally have some form of outfit ready. I took a quick shower to make sure I didn't smell like the basket of fried chicken my mom cooked. I sat in my big fluffy purple robe and decided to attempt to do something to my hair. I decided it wasn't worth the fuss and I pulled it up into a ponytail. I had a big, white, thick scrunchie that held all my braids together. I spent the next 20 minutes sitting on my mom's bed while she told me about not taking drinks from people, and the usual about sex, boys, and drugs. Little did she know, I was far from doing any drug much less any boys. I walked out of my apartment and sat on the steps as I waited for Ashley's mom to come and pick me up. Ashley's mom loved taking us out to places. I think she was reliving her youth or something. Her mom had a brand new black '96 Jeep. Ashley's mom was a housewife, and her dad owned a couple insurance agencies around town. Whenever you wanted to go shopping or have a good time, there was nothing cooler than rolling in a '96 Jeep... I sat in the front seat, a common theme due to my height. It was a little chilly still in the 50s temp-wise. I started to rethink the outfit. But I was already in the car and maybe it's a party where everyone will be dressed up. After I got in the car, we pulled off and headed to the party listening to "Hit Me Off" by New Edition. This felt so exciting.

Jason's home wasn't too far from my house. It was about a 15-minute drive. His home was like everybody else's in Jeffersonville, a 2-story home with a basement and a huge back yard. A pool was in the back too and had the nicest blue lights you could ever see. It looked like the ocean with deep, dark blue at the bottom and sky blue at the top. We could see it riding up to the house. Jess, Ashley, Shelly, and I got out of the car and went over to ring the doorbell. The driveway was super long, and I was dang near out of breath by the time I got to the door. While waiting you could hear Bone-Thugs-N Harmony and Biggie's "Notorious Thugs" banging from the inside. We did a quick look over to make sure we looked good. Jess had on a dark blue Mets baseball jersey with a black tube top underneath, dark denim blue jeans, and black and white Jordans. She also had her hair in a ponytail, but the back half was down. Ashley and Shelly were arguing back and forth because they both decided to wear Tommy Hilfiger windbreakers and they both had on black Reeboks. Ashley's was red and Shelly's was white. I began to regret my outfit as everyone was so trendy with designer labels and here I was in a summer dress and a fall shirt. So much for my mom's fashion IQ.

Some random short guy they called Philly answered the door and he looked us over like we were a two piece and a biscuit. We walked through the house and Jason had a similar style home as Jess with a big open style living room and a big floor model TV. The basement was where the party was. You could hear the bass bumping through the walls as we walked down the stairs to the basement. Jason had a big leather sectional in the middle of the floor. There was also a tall red bar in the corner next to the stereo system. There was a huge open space to dance. There wasn't a DJ, but one of the Junior Varsity guys was picking the CDs. With raised eyebrows, I glanced over, and Mike had pulled Jess away to go dance. Ashley and Shelly told me they were going to the bathroom to check their makeup, as if we hadn't just checked 15 minutes ago. I was left alone near the bar watching people dancing to *Red Light Special* by TLC like they needed a bedroom nearby. If this was the party, I could be at home watching *Moesha* or some other teen romance show. I just leaned up against the bar, next to the bowl of Cheetos.

Ashley walked over to me and asked, "Mon, can you believe this

24

party is so packed?"

I said, "Yep, everybody was saying how it was gonna be phat." I was secretly thinking this was my arrival into popularity. I mean, all the football players and important people at Jeffersonville were here. Ashley said, "Come on girl let's go dance." I thought, *ok this I can do*. I could really dance. I danced all the time in my living room to all sorts of music.

As I walked to the dance floor, I started with the basic two step. The song was a medium tempo, so I kept it cute. Shelly was on the floor as well, dancing with one of the football team players. Then they played "Time for the Percolator", a really fast paced house music song. I danced so hard my ponytail full of braids was flopping to the side. It was so much fun I almost forgot that I was now dancing alone. Ashley was to the right with some guy dancing. I stopped to look around to see if anyone was going to walk up to me and dance. I started two stepping off the floor and I felt someone touch the small of my back. This was it, my first dance at a party with a guy. I started to sway my hips a little faster and I felt him press his hand against my back even harder. So, I danced harder.

Whoever it was, leaned close to my ear and whispered, "Hey excuse me, can I get by?"

I said, "Um, sure, sorry." I was horrified, just when I thought my popularity was on the rise, I was reminded that I was just the tag along.

The guy went over to dance with some junior from school. I went back to the bar and just people-watched for a while. Jess and Mike looked happy in the corner dancing. Ashley and Shelly were somewhere on the dance floor with the rest of the cheer team. I began to wonder where Jason was. I mean, it was his party. I found a seat near the sliding doors next to the pool. I pretended to be looking for something in my purse when someone said, "Is everything ok?"

I looked up slowly and met with his eyes and said, "Yea, I am good, just thought I lost my house keys." He said, "You sure?" I quickly placed my head back down. I didn't even feel pretty enough to respond, so I just shook my head. He walked away and I thought, wow, my first encounter with the star football player Jason. I walked over to Jess and Mike and that guy, Philly, stepped in front of me causing me to stumble.

I said to him, "What do you want, boy?"

He said to me, "I'm trying to dance with you, girl." Before I could say no, he started dancing all up on me, hands waving crazy in the air. He was even popping his 'lil booty on me. Everyone was laughing at Philly. I kept thinking, although I got a dance, why did it have to be with a guy who is half my size and short. He also had the worst breath in the free world. *Man whyyyyyy?!*

My night was a bust and I couldn't wait for Ashley's mom to come back. I told Jess that I was going to sit by the pool and chill. It had turned a little cold, and everyone was inside of the party. There was a small little pool chair right near the edge where no one could see me. I began to write in my little journal that I kept in my purse. I was writing anything down just to have the appearance of looking occupied.

I heard someone say, "What are you writing?"

I said with a confused look, "Jason?" I just stared at him, he was so tall, and he was wearing this over-sized FUBU sweater with baggy blue jeans. He wore this cute little red beanie hat and had on a small gold chain with a cross.

He asked me, "You don't like parties, huh?"

I said, "I mean, yeah, I like 'em, I am here, ain't I?" I gave him a 'lil 'tude. I was so nervous that's all I could do. I changed the subject and asked, "How is chemistry?"

He said, "It's alright, but man the teacher be trippin'." We spent the next couple minutes talking about the teacher and how we thought she was monotone. Jason sat down in the chair next to me.

"So, how you like Jeffersonville so far?"

I gave him a half smile. "It's cool. The people are a little neurotic about their grass, but that's life, you know." I was getting lost in his fragrance.

"So, Jason, what's it like here from your perspective? You seem to have a lot of friends."

Jason looked down. "I mean it's cool, I guess. I love football and all but sometimes it can be a little much. Sometimes I like to just chill." I wanted to talk more but Jason started talking about school again. It was a good conversation. Somebody played Jodeci's *"Love You for Life,"* but we kept talking. His eyes had this slight squint that could pierce steel. I was listening to Jason, but my mind drifted to the video of T-boz marrying Mr. Dalvin. I really liked this song, I wished somebody loved me like it was in the video. It was also my cousin's first dance song and they looked so happy.

"You wanna dance?" I looked up at him practically staring at him like he was some Greek God. "Yeah," but my body didn't know what to do.

He told me, "You can put your arms around my neck, you know." I did just that, and I kept my head down. I just couldn't look him in the eyes. I feared he knew I didn't have a clue of what I was doing. He even smelled good like fresh Zest soap. We danced for what felt like forever. He even sang a little of the lyrics in my ear as we swayed side to side.

"I'll give you all you had before
So come on in and close the door
Let me show you what I could be
Could you just please tell me.
Do you believe in love
And the promise that it gives
I wanna love you for life
Cause your love is why I live"

I even looked up at him and thought, *would this be it, a kiss?* But the song ended, and people were starting to walk towards the door. As the song came to an end, he said he needed to get back. I thought, *wow, I just had my first dance with a boy. Chubby Monica with a football star? It couldn't be.* He left and I went back inside to leave with my girls. On the way home, I kept quiet as I was still in shock about the dance. Jess was talking about Mike and how sweet he was tonight. Ashley and Shelly said how all the guys were whack. I just looked out the window and kept imagining my dance with Jason. I told no one what happened. Our crew decided to stay at Ashley's house since we were all exhausted. Once we got home, we all passed out within the hour. It had been a long day.

Chapter 6

The next day, I woke up around 6:00 am, being that I was an early bird. The rest of the crew was asleep. Ashley had a ridiculously pink room. I mean, everything was pink. The sheets, headboard, dresser, and rug. I didn't understand the color scheme, but Ashley felt that pink was a lucky color. She also thought that nobody could ever be sad in a pink room. I sat up and grabbed a furry pink pillow to toss at Ashley's head, but she still was knocked out. Even when the pillow hit her head. I was thinking, *Man I need to call my mom,* but I didn't want to wake the house. My dance with Jason appeared in my thoughts. I felt like silk sheets on a bed. Just smooth. I went on ahead downstairs to call my mom in Ashley's formal living room around 6:15 am. I was talking to my mom and I felt someone tap my shoulder.

I nearly jumped across the living room and whispered loudly, "Boy, you scared the crap out of me!" It was Brian, Ashley's brother.

He quickly said, "You were really scared huh." He couldn't stop laughing, so much he fell onto the couch. I was ticked because I was in my pajamas and my hair was all over the place.

I said, "What are you doing up!"

He replied snarky, "Why?"

I rolled my eyes, "Boy, whatever." He had on a black FUBU jogging suit with a little gold hoop in his left earlobe. He wore his hair cut low and was about 6'1" with perfect caramel skin. Brian had a lean, muscular build, but huge arms as he played shortstop for the baseball team. Ashley previously told me her parents were having trouble with him deciding on a college. He was starting to hang out late at night with some random girls. I guess he was coming in from the night. He played baseball and had a full ride to any college he wanted.

So, I asked, "Who was it tonight?"

He said, "Dang, girl, you all up in my business, don't worry about all that." As soon as I was about to tell his butt off, his mom came downstairs. She had on a pink robe. I remember thinking, *what is it with the pink in this family?* Mrs. Harris said, "Good morning, Monica. Brian, I need to speak with you." He said nothing and followed her upstairs. Next, I heard the door slam along with Mrs. Harris yelling at Brian. Then I heard my mom say Monica, Monica! "Oh, snap mommy," I said. I had forgotten she was on the phone.

I whispered, "How much did you hear?"

She said, "I heard nothing Monica." As nosy as my mother was, I was happy she didn't hear anything. Mommy decided I would come home later around dinner time.

I headed back up the stairs and wrote in the notebook I had at the party until the other girls woke up at noon. "Hurry up y'all, I'm so hungry," Shelly yelled. She was the southern girl who loved to eat. I never mentioned food and didn't want them to think I was greedy. We yelled in unison, "OKAY, SHELLY!" We all walked down the stairs to eat breakfast and there was a lot of food on the table. Mrs. Harris cooked pancakes, eggs, sausage, bacon, and had lots of bagels. I waited until the other girls got their food because I would eat the same amount.

They all grabbed a bunch of everything. Even though they all had a lot of food I still couldn't grab a lot. I just grabbed a bagel and said my stomach was sensitive. I figured eating at home would be more comfortable.

After breakfast, we all sat upstairs listening to new CDs. We were all dancing and singing to the Spice Girls newest song, "If You Wanna be My Lover." We just kept hitting repeat on the CD player. Our crew was so tight, and all loved the same things. We finally calmed down and discussed the party last night. First, Jess described how Mike wanted her to go to the OutKast concert. Jess was so excited she forgot that we all had a girl's day planned for my birthday.

I said, "Jess, remember that's my birthday."

She replied confused, "Oh shoot, that's right, Mon, my bad."

I said, "It's cool, I mean, it's OutKast, Jess."

She said, "No way, it's your birthday, there is no way I am missing it. He can just go with his boys." Jess was a fan of OutKast so I felt bad. She would have to turn down her date just to hang out with her best friend.

I told her, "No we can all hang out the next day for my birthday, and I can move my dinner with mom on the concert night.

She said, "You sure?"

I said, "Jess, you're my home-girl, of course, and it's freaking OutKast!" Shelly and Ashley were cool with it and continued to talk about all the guys that were straight up WHACK. Especially Philly. I asked the girls did they catch a whiff o f his breath. They all agreed it wasnt the most pleasant smell of the evening.

Everyone left around 2 pm but I didn't have to be home until 4 o'clock so Ashley and I walked the dog down the street to the park. It was a little white teacup yorkie with a pink collar named Jazzy. When we arrived at the park we just sat and talked about the upcoming cheer schedule and that we had extra practices as well.

Then she asked, "Mon you get along with your mom?"

I said, "I mean for the most part, she can be a little annoying with her stories but it's always been me and her. I asked, "Why, what's up?"

She said, "Just wondering." I sat down on the bench. "Because I never really see you and her argue."

I said, "Argue! Girl please, I like my life!"

Ashley had a half smile, "Not like that, Mon, I mean she doesn't fuss at you every five minutes."

I was confused. "Ashley what do you mean?" Jazzy started to bark at some random leaves that were blowing.

Then Ashley said, "It's just my brother gets on their nerves so much they are extra tough on me." Ashley looked somber as her curly hair blew with the wind.

"How?" Ashley described a home where she had to be perfect and that her brother's actions had made her parents unbearable.

"Every time Brian does something, I get the residual, ya know? Everything I do is under a microscope. I just want them to let me live, mistakes and all." Her parents stopped acting normal when Brian got really good at baseball and started living this image of a perfect family. It was driving Ashley crazy. As her friend, I just sat and listened until we walked back to the house. When I got there, Brian was downstairs drinking orange juice out of the carton. I didn't like him for how his mini earthquake lifestyle was causing Ashley some serious aftershocks.

He asked, raising his eyebrows, "Hey you want some?"

I said, "Gross."

He walked up to me very closely, I mean nose to nose and said, "You know you want some." I was breathless. Was this a fat joke or was he flirting? I felt like punching him. He really was arrogant. I left the kitchen and grabbed my things to head home.

I spent Sunday doing laundry with my mom and writing in my journal about the weekend. Around 7:00 pm I was alone, in my room, and drifted into a daydream about how Monday would be when I returned to school. Jason would see me in the hallway and walk up and kiss me in front of everyone. I dreamed that we would sit together at lunch and discuss our relationship and first official date. How proud he would be to tell his boys about his new fine freshman girlfriend. I sat up quickly nearly falling off my bed. Oh, how I wish it could be true. Instead, I just got up and popped in my tapes of my soap operas. At least I could live through others. I sunk down under my blanket and whisked away with *General Hospital*'s Sonny and Brenda on the tube.

I woke up early on Monday to make sure I looked a little decent. I mean, I had to make up for that out of season outfit I wore to Jason's party. My mom had gone shopping and bought me new dark denim overall pants with a new FUBU t-shirt to wear underneath. I wore my white Reeboks that my grandmother had got me for making the honor roll. I was able to make four twisties in the front of my head and leave the back down. It's amazing what you can do with braids. When I arrived at school, I walked past Jess and Mike right by her locker and talked to Ashley.

"Ash, what's wrong?" She was telling me how she completely

forgot her algebra homework and was in full panic. While she was frantically looking through her book-bag, I leaned past her and saw Jason over by the water fountain. He was so handsome.

"I'm never gonna find this assignment."

I replied, "What?" I couldn't even remember what Ashley was talking about. I said, "Hey, Ash, my bad I was just thinking about something."

She said, "It's cool, so what are you doing after cheer practice?" Every Monday after school most of my school would go to the local pizza spot, Miller's. On Mondays it was 2 dollars for a slice and drink. I told Ashley, "Yea, I think might go to Miller's." I never went because I really didn't like for people to see me eat. Just as I was about to walk away, I saw Jason walking swiftly in my direction. My heart started to race, and I started to think about the daydream I had Sunday. Could it be true? Would Jason claim me in front of everyone?

Jason said to my astonishment, "Hey, Ashley do you think Shelly will be at Miller's tonight?"

Ashley replied, "Why?" I thought, *no, no he didn't. He would not dance with me and then ask out my home girl.*

Jason said, "Just had to ask her a question." Jason walked away leaving behind the smell of zest soap.

Ashley said to me, "Shelly is gonna go nuts that Jason asked about her."

I pretended to be happy. "Yes, I bet she will." My heart felt like someone just reached in and squeezed the little hope I had left. After school I debated whether I would go to Miller's or just head home. I wouldn't be able to face Jason and Shelly if they became a couple. But on the other hand, who could resist the southern belle from South Carolina with a bangin' body? Jason was a nice guy, maybe he just danced with me to be nice. I mean, it wouldn't work anyway. I was not the girl to get asked out. I was just the *friend*.

Chapter 7

Change wasn't a big component I enjoyed in my 14 years of life. I liked things to stay the same because I knew what to expect. Jason dancing with me led to some alternate universe in TV land where I thought a chubby girl could actually date someone that didn't smell. This situation with Jason and Shelly is something I didn't see coming but I needed to know if Jason really liked Shelly so I could just place my feelings in my pocket. I needed to know even if my daydreams were a waste of time so, I went ahead to Miller's in my gold cheer joggers and blue hoodie. I blended in with the rest of the cheer team as they wore joggers too. I walked through the door and thought, *Jeez, is everyone that is an athlete in here today?* Blue and gold was everywhere. Miller's had black circle tables with black chairs. The decor on the walls was red, white, and green and paid homage to the Italian roots of the owner.

Jess said, "Hey, Mon, did you take notes today?"

I said, "Of course I did, you can borrow mine if you need to."

I reached in my book-bag to give Jess my notes and Jess asked, "Where is Shelly?" I said, "I dunno, I thought she would be here by now." I secretly hoped she wouldn't come and that way, I wouldn't have to discuss what Jason said about her today. Jess began to talk about her relationship with Mike for the hundredth time that day.

"Mike has on the cutest Fila hoodie today." As I listened, I nearly gagged. However, she appeared to really be in love with Mike.

As a good friend I asked Jess, "So, what is it about Mike that makes him so sweet?"

Jess said, "He calls me every night before bed and walks me to all my classes." Now, I had personally seen Mike with a few other girls casually, but I never said anything.

I told her, "He is really popular Jess, I mean everyone hangs around him."

Missing my subtle signal Jess said, "Girl, I know, but he is so nice he talks to everybody." Ashley chimed in and said, "I mean we are lucky, we have all these upper-class guys checking for us, it's awesome."

I said sarcastically, "Yeah, awesome."

Jess said, noticing my sarcasm, "Oh, girl, come on, I saw Philly all up on you at the party."

Rolling my eyes, "Yeah right, Philly and his breath were all up on me." The girls chuckled. I looked around and I saw Shelly come in rather chipper. Shelly sat down and ordered a pepperoni slice.

Before I could say anything, Ashley said, "So, Mon, did you tell Shelly about Jason?"

I said, "No, I was waiting for you." I was clearly lying, but I allowed her to go on with the story. Ashley told Shelly and Jess that Jason had a question for her and if she would be at Miller's. Shelly looked stunned, but happy. She actually reached over and gave me a tight side hug.

Shelly said, "I mean, wow, I had a feeling he was checking me out at the party." We spent the next hour talking about what Jason could possibly want from Shelly. We debated maybe it was about another guy

Jason wanted Shelly to meet or to simply needing help with schoolwork. It was like we all were waiting on the fate of our destiny. The star football player potentially liked someone from our crew. This would set us for years to come. As soon as we finished our last bite of food, in walked Jason and a couple of the guys from the team. Oh, and Philly. I again rolled my eyes as he walked over to my table. Philly said, "Hey, y'all, what up?" Philly grabbed a chair and sat down next to me. The girls were all smiling about Philly sitting there. His breath actually smelled decent today and it wasn't so bad sitting next to him. It dawned on me that I was treating Philly like people teased me. Now his breath did stank at the party but I didn't have to mistreat him.

Philly was in rare form, cracking jokes on everybody in the room, even Jason. I specifically enjoyed those jokes, that would teach him to diss me. In fact, I didn't realize Philly was this cool. In the middle of my laugh Jason walked over to the table. I glanced over and Shelly was literally grinning like the Grinch Who Stole Christmas only she was stealing my could be man. On the other hand, I was kind of happy, this was my friend and all.

Later on Jason eventually walked over to the table. "Hey, yall what up?" We all said Hi. "Hey, Shelly can I holler at you for a sec." They got up from the table and we all tried to play it cool. I felt like I was going to explode. I couldn't believe I had these feelings after one stupid dance. Jason and I just had a dance, not a kiss. Well, he ended up asking Shelly out for a movie this weekend and she said yes. Just as I predicted. Even though it kind of sucked I should have expected that news. When Jason and Philly left, I mouthed OH MY GOD. Our crew had arrived, but I couldn't help but wonder if Jason didn't remember our dance and why was he acting weird. That evening, I called Shelly to tell her the girls and I would come over to help her get ready for her date with Jason. The next day at school was weird. Everyone was watching us like we were the new celebs of the school. Even the upper-class girls were friendly towards us. I was getting ready to head to the field because Coach Minnie was yelling for all the girls to stretch their legs. I saw the football guys leaving the back of the school as they had a film session. Jason was lingering around talking to Mike and the guys. I had to go back into the building to grab the poms for the second half of practice.

As I walked out the door Jason walked up and asked, "You need some help?"

I said, "No, I got it." Then I asked, "So, you like my girl, huh?"

He said, "Yeah, she straight and well, you know."

I said, "Know what?" Jason just got quiet and we caught eyes. Then he touched my cheek gently almost like a feather. My heart felt like it was gonna jump out of my chest.

I said, "Jason?"

He said, "Yea?"

I said, "Is there something on my face?"

He laughed and said, "Mon, you are silly."

Chuckling I said, "So are you ready for your date?"

Jason replied looking at his feet, "I am…I mean… I guess, Shelly is cool." So, there it was, he only danced with me because he was being nice. I decided then that I would be a good friend and help them both with getting their relationship off the ground. I walked back to practice feeling good about my friends and I was happy.

Right after practice, Coach Minnie and I were going over what the cheer team would be wearing for homecoming. Shelly and Jess came running over to me like they had won something.

Shelly said, "Girl, Jason asked me if you want to double with us this Saturday."

I said, "With who, girl?"

She said, "Philly." My eyes got extremely large. Even Coach Minnie did a side chuckle.

I said, "Nope, are you crazy? He is like 5'6 or 7 and one case of good breath doesn't make a date." Coach Minnie really started laughing.

Shelly said, "Come on, Mon, I need a buffer, this is my first date here, in town, and I'm really nervous."

I said, "Shelly, look, he is just too short."

She said, "Ok, if you go, I will do your algebra homework for a week." I was no dummy, but I hated math with a vengeance, and she knew it. But I was no cheater.

I said, "Ok, Shelly, I will think about it." She gave me the biggest hug it almost took my breath away.

The next day at school I was standing near my locker getting my books out. I stood a little bit longer thinking about Philly and maybe it wouldn't be so bad. At least I would have a date, and it would be the first one. Just as I was about to freak out a little bit, Jess came walking up to my locker.

I said, "Jess, hey did you still want to link up later?"

Jess replied, "Yea, girl I do." Her eyes were downcast, and she looked so sad.

I said, "Jess, what is wrong?" She just looked at me. I pulled her by her denim jacket down the hall. She didn't even try and resist. I tried to begin the conversation and then Mike came running down the hall yelling to get our attention.

"Jess!...Yo, Jess!" Mike placed his arms around Jess's waist, only this time she didn't look happy. I was used to them being all over each other. Now, she looked defeated as if she was standing in a desert in need of water. That was not like my confident friend who didn't take crap off nobody. I'd had it with Mr. Mike.

I stared Mike down what seemed like forever, "What did you do to her, Mike?"

He looked at me confused and said, "What you talking about, girl?"

I folded my arms and pointed my eyes like they were military missiles ready to fire and said, "You tell me, MIKE!" I wasn't the most popular, but I was nobody's punk when it came to my family and friends, and neither was Jess. I couldn't understand this silent version of my best friend.

"Why do you care, you not my woman."

I replied, "But she is my home-girl and I have her back and something looks wrong." I backed up a couple feet because I felt a rush of anger brewing. For someone who never had a real fight, I was ready for Mike to feel the years of bullying I endured.

But his narrow self wasn't worth it and I told him, "Mike I don't want no drama ok; I just want to make sure she is good." Mike then attempted to give me a serious look like I was his child.

"Look M-O-N-I-C-A." He pronounced every syllable of my name. "Jess is not your business and she is fine. So, butt out and stop hatin'.'" Just as I was about to tell his butt off for good.

Jess blurted out. "Mon, just leave it alone ok, I got this!" I stood there, arms folded, biting my lip.

"Fine." I left for class.

Once I got to class, she passed me a note. I didn't want to read it because there were too many nosy people in the room. I looked up at the clock while the teacher was explaining about the school play that we could audition for next spring. It would be a remake of *Romeo and Juliet*. Usually, upperclassmen were only allowed to audition for lead roles. This year all classes could audition. In reality, nobody was really into Shakespeare, so they opened the field. I already thought I would audition for the nurse role. I loved that part, a loyal friend to Juliet and available to listen. The bell rang and I headed down the hall for Keyboarding class. The teacher was usually late, so I lingered by the door to read Jessica's note.

Hey, Mon

I didn't appreciate you embarrassing me like that in the hallway with Mike. I know I looked sad and all but it's between Mike and myself. We had a small argument before class about some junior girl. No big deal. You acted like my dang momma. Hovering over me. I mean I guess you don't know what it's like to have a boyfriend. So, I understand. Look, I am cool just let me handle Mike ALRIGHT.

See you later bestie.

I stared at the paper for what felt like hours. Reading it over and over to see if there was some misunderstanding for being straight up rude. Jess made me feel like an outsider and I was fired up. I kept thinking, *I was only trying to help Jessica and be a good best friend.* I balled up the letter and threw it in the trash bin next to Keyboarding class. The rest of the day I couldn't really focus between thinking about this awful date Saturday and Jessica's note. I just didn't know what to say to Jess. Should I apologize or tell her she hurt my feelings? I generally had no problem telling somebody to shut up. But, being in Jeffersonville, I had a fresh group of friends and decided it wasn't worth the fight. Plus, I actually cared about my friendship. When I arrived at cheer practice everyone was still in the locker room. Jess hadn't gotten there; she was in the hallway talking to Mr. Mike. In the locker room, all the upper-class cheerleaders were talking about their boyfriends. They were discussing all the important relationships at Jefferson High. Then I heard Mike's name come up and some girl named Nikki. I was standing behind the lockers while they talked. The girls didn't even notice me.

Our captain Melody said, "Yo, Mike and Jess were fighting hard over Nikki y'all." Melody continued while getting dressed. "Nikki and Mike were at Miller's talking pretty close and shared some pizza from what I hear."

Another cheerleader said, "Girl, I heard they left together." Coach Minnie came in looking for some poms and the girls stopped their conversation. Coach looked ticked off so I ducked down behind the lockers so the girls couldn't see me as they left. Jess and the crew came in late. Jess still looked upset, but I just left it alone because practice was about to be brutal enough. I never liked Mike, but she made it clear in her letter that I had no place in discussing their relationship. I stood up and walked onto the gym floor after everyone left the locker room as if I heard nothing.

Chapter 8

———— ◄◆◆► ————

Practice was really long today, and the cheerleaders were working really hard for homecoming next weekend. Once everyone got to the floor, Coach Minnie gave this annoying monologue about being responsible. "Girls, if you can't be on time...yadda yadda." I sat on the bleachers and watched Coach have them redo the stunt over and over until it was perfect. I personally felt she was punishing them for gossiping and being late for practice. However, it was this one girl Nicole that just had a horrible attitude for no reason. She was a junior and walked around the school like her stuff didn't stank. Nicole was about 5'5" feet tall and had this horrible blonde hair that was shoulder length. You could tell the bleach used to dye her hair was left in her hair too long because it was fried, stringy, and thin. She had a rather slim build with a small dimple in each cheek. She always wore these earrings with her name plated in the middle like every girl in the school didn't have the same earrings. I mean, this girl was just straight up nasty in my opinion. I remember a time when someone wrote a snippet in the school's newspaper about some sophomore's sexual infection history all because her ex-boyfriend started dating the girl. Nicole had a crew of people that were sort of cool and tried to keep her in check. The thing about Nicole was she wasn't a loud bully. She was a sneaky, lowdown, sniper. She would attack like a slithering snake from behind. She was too uppity to hang out with any high school guys, she only dated college boys. It was sad that I knew of her reputation from only being in Jeffersonville a few months. It was also sad that Nicole aka Nikki was the girl that Mike was supposedly cheating on Jess with at Miller's. At practice, she started to complain about being at practice too long to Coach. I didn't understand why the other girls tolerated her. She said, "Dang, Coach, we've been here forever, how long we gone stay?!"

One of the girls whispered, "She prolly trying to meet up with Mike." It dawned on me that this was the Nikki they were gossiping about.

Nikki continued letting out a deep sigh that could fill up a car tank, "We got it, dang coach!" Some of the girls chuckled but quickly stopped when they saw Coach Minnie got up from her chair and shot Nikki a death stare. But that Nikki just kept going, as if Coach was a joke.

Nikki said under her breath, "I bet you Coach ain't had a date since the 80s, she clearly has no life." I knew with Nikki saying that Coach was going to explode if she heard it, but she didn't, I guess. All she said was, "Practice is over." We all looked shocked, with our mouths open and complied with Coach's request. I was thinking that darn Nikki was something else. She was able to shut Coach Minnie up, which was quite a feat seeing as she talked and fussed every 5 minutes. I hoped Coach wasn't going soft because even though she was a motormouth our team was the bomb because of her tough ways. I left practice with Shelly so I could get ready for our date at her house with Jason and Philly.

I sat in Shelly's room and looked around at all the trophies. It looked like a sporting goods store had exploded in her room. She had a vanity where she sat to get ready for the date. Her walls were an off-white color with one powder blue accent wall. Shelly had on a black satin robe while she curled her hair. I walked over to help curl her hair and then 3 little monsters came running in the room like they were on a freakin' sugar high. The kids were 6, 4, and 2. They were jumping all over the bed and trying to get Shelly's attention.

I asked, "Shelly, what's up with your siblings, man?"

I continued, "We never gonna get ready if they keep on jumping everywhere." Shelly yelled at them and they left. I thought I loved kids, but I can't stand bad ones. I mean, they just work my whole central nervous system. We turned on some music to continue getting ready. "Hey let's turn on some Faith Evans." Shelly looked at me sideways as she was stuck in rumorville about Faith and Tupac, and loved Biggie.

"Girl you better let that stuff go, Faith is the bomb. Plus I wanna hear Soon as I get home. You know you got the tape."

"Whatever, it's over there" Shelly was starting to look nervous.

Shelly said, "Well how does my hair look?"

I said, "Girl, Jason is gonna love it."

Shelly said, "You gonna wear your hair up or down?" I had gotten it re-braided into long box braids the other day. My mom didn't believe in super short anything she felt it was against a woman's religion.

I said, "I think I'm gonna wear it up in a ponytail."

Shelly said, "Yea, that's gonna be cute." Shelly laid her outfit on the bed and it was black jeans with a sleeveless turtleneck shirt and square heeled black boots. I wasn't particularly thrilled about this date, so I just wore some blue jeans with a navy-blue bodysuit and a black vest. Had to cover my little pudge. I wore black flat shoes; I mean Philly nearly came to my chin so a heel would be crazy.

I asked Shelly, "So what are you looking for in Jason?"

She replied, "I mean, I dunno, he popular and I guess that means he cool. Besides, he is FINE, girl!" Then she said, "Plus he seems nice and everything, you know. He volunteers and stuff I hear." That southern accent was in full mode.

I said, "Yea, he seems cool, but just take your time, you know." Shelly replied while looking in her vanity and primping her hair, "I will Mon."

Jason's car was a '95 Jeep that he got on his 16th birthday over the summer. I hoped that I didn't have that awkward seat adjustment when getting into the car. Tall and thick girls sometimes have that issue when folks think they have to ride in the front seat of the car. People just assume because you're tall or thick that it means you ride up front. Although it was true it still sucked having that awkward silence while you're trying to figure out who sits where. We sat downstairs to wait for Jason and Philly along with Shelly's parents. Our date was scheduled for 7 pm and the boys arrived right on time. The doorbell rang and I suddenly felt a little nervous. Shelly's mom answered the door and talked to the guys about curfew and rules. But my eyes were stuck on Philly, he looked like one of those hype men in the rap videos. He wore a bright blue FUBU jersey with a red cap along with light denim jeans. I simply couldn't do it, this was horrible. Jason had on a black Pelle Pelle turtleneck with dark denim jeans and a fresh pair of Lugz boots. While I was rethinking this whole date, Shelly was grinning from ear to ear and gave Jason this big hug. I looked over at Philly and my feet felt like cement in the floor, I was frozen. Shelly looked at me and said, "Come on, girl, we are gonna be late for the movie."

Philly said, "Come on, girl, let's roll, you with Big Philly tonight." I thought to myself, *BIG my foot.* The weather was about 59 degrees this evening with a beautiful moon. Jason kept turning the radio and finally put in the 112 tape of "Only You". Philly asked me had I seen *The Nutty Professor* yet. I told him no. That was it, no conversation after that, we just rode in silence. I glanced up and I saw Jason looking in the rear-view mirror at us, with a smirk on his face. Philly reached over and asked, "Hey you ok? You're so quiet." I thought this was nice of Philly to care to ask.

I responded, "Yes, I am ok just a little tired from the week, ya know." We rode the rest of the way debating over who was the best rapper Tupac or Biggie seeing as Tupac was killed only the month prior. Shelly mostly looked in the mirror checking her lipstick every 5 minutes. We pulled into the parking lot of the Jeffersonville Movie Theater and both guys opened the door for Shelly and me. The good thing is the movie aired over the summer and most of our classmates had seen the movie and weren't there tonight. Philly mentioned everyone went to the bowling alley. Walking in Philly bought my ticket and popcorn and drinks. I was surprised at how nice Philly was being. He actually brushed his teeth. Shelly was getting butter for their popcorn while Philly and I waited at the door. Walking into the movie, Jason and Philly were debating on where to sit. Philly wanted to sit up front and Jason wanted to sit in the back.

I said, "Look guys, let's just sit in the middle, that way you both win, yeesh." Sitting through the movie was actually cool and the movie was quite funny. Eddie Murphy had outdone himself. I told Philly I was going to the bathroom, but in reality, I just needed a breather from seeing Shelly and Jason. If I was going to be a good friend, I would have to keep myself together. In the bathroom I looked in the mirror and just stared at myself thinking, *you can do this, Mon.* I walked out of the restroom and back into the movie. I heard some guys laughing obnoxiously hard near the back of the theater. I turned around with my face scrunched up giving the guys a look that would kill. I squinted my eyes, and I noticed a small gold hoop earring in one of the guys ears. I wondered if it was Brian, but it couldn't be, he was always attached to the lips of some chick. This evening he was with the baseball team, who in my opinion, were a bunch of jerks. They walked the halls like they were untouchable. I couldn't stand how they always picked on people who they considered lame. The noise didn't seem to bother Philly and I didn't want to interrupt Shelly's date.

I whispered to Philly, "Hey, ain't this noise bothering you?"

Philly replied, "I mean not really, they just laughing at the movie."

I said, "The heck they are, Philly they are laughing at parts that aren't even funny. They are being butts." Philly said, "Look I don't want no trouble, so just chill." Sitting there I understood Philly was just scared of losing his rep. Although, his breath was much better he was decent looking. He still didn't want to ruin his potential popularity. I sat there and just cringed in my seat through the rest of the movie while Brian and crew sounded like a bunch of idiots laughing every 2 seconds. As the movie ended, we all walked to the lobby. Jason and Shelly were talking about how funny the movie was and Philly tried to imitate

Professor Klump. Philly kept clapping his hands saying, 'Cleatus, Cleatus.' I was cracking up. The date turned out nicely. The boys went to get the car while Shelly and I talked about how Jason was so nice to her and held her hand in the movie. Just when Jason honked for us to go to the car, Brian came up behind me and this time he grabbed my waist tickling me. I hated being tickled because my cousins would tickle me until I had to go to the restroom. Brian doing it made him even more annoying.

I said, "Brian, you not funny, so stop doing that crap."

Brian said, "Girl, I'm just playing. Anyway, you and Shelly need a ride?"

I said, "Why you assume we came alone?" I could see Jason staring out of his window looking annoyed. Brian came back around to my face, "Ohhh, so you on a date? Where is homeboy at? Let me check him out." Brian was looking around for my date.

"Not that it's any of your business but I came with Philly and Shelly came with Jason." Brian's whole crew started laughing.

"Philly... Really? That sophomore dude is crazy man." Brian added.

I just rolled my eyes. Brian walked over, grabbed my waist and whispered in my ear, "I would have taken you out."

"Look, boy." I pushed him back and crossed my arms, then I looked around the car to see if Philly saw anything, but Philly was busy bopping his head to the music.

Shelly said, while looking irritated. "Girl, come on, the guys are waiting."

I said sharply, "Brian, goodbye."

Walking across the street, Shelly said, "Girl, what was that stuff with Brian? Does Ashley know about this?"

I replied, "Girl, Brian just being a jerk per usual. He got so many girls it's not even funny. He just a flirt is all."

"Oh, ok yeah you're probably right. He hangs with all the girls. He probably want your help with something." Boy I tell you, being chubby, people automatically assume you're the tutor. Shelly and I got into the car and talked about the movie some more on the way home, but Jason was awkwardly quiet. Philly and I laughed and laughed. Even while Jason was shooting mean looks in the rearview mirror, we managed to enjoy the evening. Pulling up in front of Shelly's you could see her mom looking through the curtains so when the guys walked us to the door there was no funny business. I told Philly I would call him tomorrow and Jason told Shelly he would call when he made it home. I said, "Goodbye, guys, maybe next time we do a game night or something." Philly was excited but Jason just kept walking to the car. Shelly was even perplexed about the end of the date. Shelly and I went into the house and chatted about the movie a little. Once we got upstairs away from the demon children, we called Ashley and Jess to discuss the date. Shelly felt like the date was ok and didn't mind another one. The only thing she hated was that her parents were being extra by looking through the curtains. Which, I didn't understand, but parents would be parents. I knew that Philly and I would be better off as friends and I think Philly knew too. But it was still my first date. I pulled out my journal to document the evening along with my big purple robe and I must say it wasn't a bad experience. Philly, I hoped would understand that we were better off as friends and Shelly and Jason would become a couple.

I woke up the next morning and waited downstairs for my mom to pick me up from Shelly's. When I got to the car, she was so excited I could barely get hello out before she started grilling me. Mom took me to a local spot called Jonies Pancakes to discuss my first date. I told my mom I thought of Philly as a friend, but she couldn't stop grinning. Her hair was a little frizzy from her early morning workout and that made it hard for me to take her seriously without laughing. It looked like she stuck her finger in a socket. But my mom seemed to be on a Philly campaign for marriage.

She said, "I mean he seems so nice."

I said, "Mom pleasssse, you haven't even met him."

She said, "Well he seems like a nice boy." She went on to tell me that nice boys were rare as teenagers and to give Philly a chance.

I responded, "Mom, Philly isn't my type and besides we clicked more as friends."

Mom said, "Well just give it a chance and you will see."

I said, "Mommy, he is just too short and he, sometimes, has bad breath."

Mom huffed scratching her frizzy hair, "Sometimes you have to take a little bad to get to something great." I began to get angry; I mean, did she think I wasn't good enough to get a guy who had good breath 100 percent of the time? My mom sensed my change in attitude.

"Monica is there a problem?" I should have answered yes and told her how she made me feel like crap, but I quickly got happy because she was not the "ONE" and I secretly felt maybe she was right. When I got home from breakfast, I pondered going over to Jess's house to talk about the letter, but I couldn't stop thinking of the words, YOU DON'T HAVE A BOYFRIEND and my mom echoing that I should accept less, it was just too much. I just went on with the day and organized my things for school.

Chapter 9

I t was finally here, HOMECOMING! Jefferson High celebrated homecoming by having a Spirit Week and ending with a class hall decorating contest. The sophomores were talking smack because they won in '95. However, our freshman class had decided to go with a M & M theme to represent the class of 2000.

The first day of the week was 70s day and my mom helped me find a red sizzler dress in my aunt's closet. That's another word for a mini dress and I wore brown knee boots with the dress. I was lucky my aunt kept everything; she was slightly thick in high school so it worked out. I had to get to school early to put up the signs in freshman hall since I recently signed up to be on the Freshman Student Council committee. Jess had been elected Freshman Class President and I signed up to help even though she ticked me off. I was standing in a chair and saw Jason and his friends walking down the hall. Jason told them he would catch up as they went down the stairs. I was climbing off the step stool and I asked Jason to come over so I could talk about the date.

I whispered, "Soooo, how did you like the date with Shelly?" He just stood there quiet with his hands on his book bag straps.

I asked again, "Hellooo, Jasonnnn, Shelly, Date?"

He finally spoke, "Man, what's up with you and Brian?"

Now, I was the silent one. He then harshly said, "Brian, really?

You were on a date and you couldn't wait until Philly didn't see you?" I stood there staring at him confused. He nearly dragged me by the arm into the nearby classroom and slammed the door shut. Now I was ready to fire back,

"Jason, first of all, Philly didn't see me. Second of all, Brian and I didn't do anything. Third of all it's none of your freaking business."

"It is my business," Jason said.

"How?" I said. Jason started to turn beet red.

"I mean Philly liked you and you gonna flirt with another guy?" Jason asked.

"Look, Jason I talked to Philly the next day and we agreed friendship was best, even though it's none of your business." I said sternly.

"Where do you get off telling me I can't talk to someone, Jason?" He got quiet. All you could hear were the birds chirping outside of the window. I was steaming mad. He probably could see fire coming from my mouth. Not only had he dissed me for my friend now he was accusing me of playing Philly. I decided to reserve my friendly fire.

I calmly said, "Look Jason I don't have to sit here and take this ok? Philly is cool so......" I turned to walk out of the door, but he pulled me back by the edge of my skirt. Before I knew it, his mouth covered over mine. I was in shock. I didn't know how to respond to the kiss so, I puckered my lips and kissed him back. He grabbed my face with both hands and kissed me some more. I couldn't believe it...I was kissing a boy and he smelt so good.... like Zest soap. I snapped out of it quickly as I thought about Shelly.

As I was catching my breath, I said, "Jason what are we doing?

What about Shelly?" Jason moved in to kiss me again, but I moved my face. I sat down at a desk and asked, "Jason where is this coming from? I'm so confused." Jason said nothing and he just stood there looking flustered breathing heavily.

I stated while looking at him confused, "What about the party? The dance we shared? Why did you ask out my friend?" I ran those questions like a speed round of jeopardy.

He said, "Mon, look, I don't know what this is, and it's hard for me, and Shelly is pop…"

I cut him off and walked close to his face and said, "Popular I know, so you can't date me, right?" He said nothing just looked at me with this look of hurt and fear. I couldn't believe we were in a full argument and not even a couple. Jason kept talking to me about popularity and although I was cool, his friends wouldn't understand. Also, that he only went out with Shelly because his friends thought it would be a good look. I turned my back to him. This conservation felt emotionally exhausting.

"Look, Jason, I get it, you are nervous about your friends."

My eyes started to water up. "But you don't understand how that makes me feel, you can only dance and kiss me in private. I am not a secret, Jason."

He stared at me looking sad, "MON, I know…I just can't." Jason searched my eyes for understanding. Almost as if he wanted this to continue in private. Heck I was contemplating this in my head during the whole argument. I mean it was better than nothing. But I knew better.

"Jason if you can't deal with me in public then we should keep this kiss and dance as a secret and I will be your friend."

"Mon can't we just kick it for now, I'm just not ready." He was practically begging me at this point. I had esteem issues, but I was no dummy. I said, "Jason, I am gonna leave now." I got up from the chair and he tried to keep me there by blocking the door. I wanted to hug him and tell him I would accept the arrangement. Thinking maybe this would be the best I could have until he was ready. My mom would agree, but my stupid eyes started welling with tears. I really didn't want him to see me cry as it was becoming a regular occurrence with the people in my life. "Please, move, Jason. I just want to be alone." He moved to the side and I left the room. Walking to the restroom, my blue eye-shadow that I had on earlier was sweated off and my lipstick had evaporated. I looked in the mirror and started to doubt myself. I had gone through a lot this past week. It started with that letter from Jess, then my mom wanting me to settle with Philly, and finally Jason being afraid to be seen with me. This chubby girl was tired. I stayed in the restroom stall for another 15 minutes and just cried. Some Spirit Week.

After school that day, I went to Miller's and I was just exhausted from all of the drama from the day. I just wanted to sit in my feelings and eat a slice of pizza alone, but then Jess and Mike came strolling in and sat down at my table. I immediately had a frown on my face, as I was in no freaking mood to deal with Jess and Mike's mess. Mike actually went over and sat with some of the football team and Jess started to talk.

She asked, "So, Mon, how you been?" I said sharply, "FINE."

"Ok," Jess said. "Look, Mon, I know that letter may have seemed harsh, but I just wanted to handle Mike on my own. I also love you very much and you are my friend…I don't want us to fight."

I sat upright in my chair, "Jess, I love you as well, it's ok." I chose to not say anything, I was afraid I would lose her as a friend. It's no fun being an outsider in high school. Jess and I continued to talk, and I told her about my date with Philly and also about the upcoming Homecoming dance. We finally were on good terms again. I finished my pizza in front of Jess without fear of feeling fat that day. In addition, I knew my boundaries in her relationship.

Friday was school spirit day, and we all wore blue and gold. In addition, the pep rally would be in the afternoon. The game would be after school and the dance would be the next day. I chose to skip the dance simply because I wasn't asked, and I was over it. When the pep rally was set to start all of the cheerleaders had to arrive early. I was kind of tired from filling in for Nikki who was

suspended for a week due to yelling at the coach. It turned out after a lot of practice I wasn't a half bad base and my jumps were so much better. My captain Melody was a good coach in helping me learn the steps. Entering the hallway, I noticed that Nikki wasn't there, and Coach Minnie asked me to come to her office.

She said, "Hey, Johnson, are you ready to suit up?"

I said, "Suit up for what? I'm dressed for the prep-rally."

"You're my newest Jeffersonville Highschool Cheerleader." Coach said.

"What about Nikki?" I questioned.

"Well Nikki isn't going to be returning." My mouth dropped.

"And…we were really impressed with your passion with this team, sooo you're in if you want too." Coach replied. I nearly jumped into her arms and knocked her down when I accepted. Soon after, I ran into the restroom to put on my cheer uniform. I prayed to God that it fit. I pulled my blue cheer shirt on and it fit perfectly. Next, was the bright gold pleated skirt. I had to squeeze a little bit into the skirt, but it actually fit. I bent over and jumped up and down before I left to make sure I didn't have an embarrassing moment. Coach Minnie lined us up in the hallway and she announced I was the newest member of the squad and the girls literally jumped on top of me. As we ran into the gym I started waving my blue and gold poms in the air like I just hit the lottery. We started our chant. JEFFERSON...Clap...Clap...Cougars. I was smiling so wide they could sit on the top of the bleachers. The football team ran in through the super large banner with Jville written across the top. Jason turned around and winked at me. I just shook my head.

Chapter 10

---◆—◆—◆---

We won the homecoming game, so we all went to Mike's to celebrate the win. The cheer team all carpooled with the upperclassmen to the party which was nice. Everyone had a chance to switch outfits and shower after the game. I wore a red long sleeve shirt with a black skirt to the ankles and black lace up boots. My earrings were silver hoops with a matching silver bracelet. This party was mostly chill with just the football team and cheerleaders. Shelly was talking my ear off about her plans for the dance. But I kept thinking about Jason kissing me and how I wanted to tell Shelly, but I couldn't. I didn't want to hurt her feelings. I went and sat at the spades table with Jess, we were FIRE at Spades. Nobody would play with us because they said we cheated, but this time we would play with Jason and Mike. As the hands were dealt, I started an interesting conversation on cheating in relationships.

While searching my hand I asked, "Sooo, what do you all define as cheating?" Everyone looked at me as if I asked a foreign question. Mike responded quick as lightning,

"Um let's change the subject." I dropped the topic and focused on my hand. I know Jess was relieved I did, but I was really still hurt from that letter. At this point, I just wanted to move on. Mike continued after drinking his soda...

"Anyway, bro what happened with you and Shelly are y'all kickin' it or what?" Mike asked while dealing another hand of cards. I was personally watching Jason's response to this question like a hawk. "Ay, you know, we cool man." Jason said while sorting his hand trying to avoid the matter.

"Well, man you need to snatch her up its plenty of brothers waiting in line." I played another card to move the game along.

"Y'all gone hang again or what?" Jason looked annoyed at the question, but I wanted to know too.

"Yes, Jason, are you guys going to hang." I said in my proper voice. Jason shot me a 'don't you even go there with me look'. In fact, I am sure Shelly would date him as she really liked him. She had had no clue of Jason secretly liking me or whatever this thing is with us. I still, for some reason, hoped he would just accept me. But since that wasn't going to happen, I at least knew if he couldn't have me, it wouldn't be Shelly either. Then out of nowhere, Jason drops a bomb right on my heart.

"Well man, I just asked her to the Homecoming Dance." I looked over at Jess to appear excited. "What she say, bro?" Mike asked. Jess looked excited and gently kicked me under the table.

"She said, yes, of course." Jason said being extra like he was some 70s mack.

"Hey, man that's my home-girl you talking about." Jess sternly replied.

"My bad, Jess, I was just playing, man." Jason had my blood boiling at this point, but I just kept playing cards slapping them down every hand.

"Hey, Mon, why don't you go with Philly?" Jess was pushing that mess again.

"No, I am gonna stay home." You would have thought the world ended by looking at their faces. "Girl, why?" Jess continued to play like what I was saying was nonsense.

"You coming, matter of fact, you can come with Mike and I."

Mike, not even looking up from his hand said, "Oh no, Mike don't do extras." Jess rolled her eyes.

"Yes, we do" Jess pushed back placing her hand over Mike's cards.

"It's cool, Jess. I have a lot of things to catch up on, plus my mom and I have something planned."

"You sure, girl?" Jess looked at my eyes to make sure.

"I'm sure, Jess," I got up and went towards the bathroom and Jason tried to corner me. "Monica, look I didn't mean for you to find out that way." I kept walking as if I didn't hear a word he was saying. He just stood there holding his red solo cup. After that exchange, I went over to talk with Ashley and Shelly and to ask about the dance.

"Hey Ash, are you going to the dance tomorrow?"

"Yep, going with Eric." Eric was our school's resident popular nerd, but he was cool.

"What about you, huh? Philly maybe." Ashley was elbowing me in the side.

"Nope, just gonna hang out at home and relax." I went and stood next to Shelly. Ashley put her soda down on the table.

"Oh, no you're not, you're going." Ashley was slightly frustrated.

"Yep, I second that, we still have time to find you a date, Mon." Shelly placed her hand on my shoulder.

"As a matter of fact, I know Philly wanted to ask you, but he wasn't sure you wanted to go with him." I was getting annoyed with Shelly and Ashley.

"Guys look, I just don't want to go ok? Can you please let this go?" I pleaded with them to just leave it alone, I wasn't a charity case for Pete's sake. After that conversation, I kind of disappeared into the party. Jason kept coincidentally staring at me as if he needed to talk but I was done. I was in the friend zone and that was it. Somehow, I slid out the back door unnoticed and I went home, there was too much drama for the night.

On Saturday mornings, I would get up, clean the house, and then just relax. My mom was out doing retail therapy. When she was stressed, she counselled herself with her credit card. I just laid in the bed and watched my soaps from the week. I briefly thought about the homecoming dance but then I realized I would be fine. Just when I was about to take a nap, the phone rang.

"Hey, why you leave the party like that." I paused as I couldn't believe this person had the nerve to call me. I thought, *why he was calling me and how did he get my number?* I had to think quickly,

"I was just tired, that's all." I attempted to get comfortable in my bed.

"Oh, ok tired, huh." Jason was questioning my reasons, that boy could read me like a book.

"Ok, Jason I guess I was a little tired of hearing about my home girl and you and whatever this thing is between us." I threw the ball back in his court.

"Monica, you know the spot I'm in, the guys expect me and Shelly to be the new power couple here." "Power couple, huh?" I asked while laughing.

"I can't go against the crew, you know." That comment sent me to 10.

I screamed in the phone, "Jason, WHY THE HECK ARE YOU CALLING FOR THEN?"

"Monica, calm down, I just wanted to explain the Shelly situation." He was trying to sooth me with his deep voice.

"Are you trying to make me feel bad, Jason?" I was hurt. It felt like I was being dumped before I even had a date. We just held the phone breathing heavily for a while. I wanted to be in Jason's life, but I wouldn't be a secret and I wouldn't betray my homie. So, I came up with a solution. I calmed down to a 7.

"Ok, Jason...You listening?"

"Yes, Monica, I am listening." "Jason, I understand you're deal with friends and stuff so, like I said before, let's just be cool friends. Plus, I don't want to hurt Shelly, she really likes you." I heard nothing from the other end of the phone "Jason?...Jason?"

"Yea, I'm here" He said, sounding sad.

"Well, what do you think." I was pushing him to answer. "Yes, friends are fine. I mean... I know how important your friends are to you, Mon." He actually was thinking of me. Holding the phone to my ear, I wished I could be smaller because Jason is a great guy. I changed my attitude. "Jason it's cool, Shelly will be happy, and you get your "dream girl" and I keep my friends." I said it with some laughter. My feelings were still hurt but I had to move on. We spent the next couple of hours just talking as friends. I got to know about his family and how they were really excited about his football stuff. He also had some fears about people just using him for clout. I shared with him about my mom and I and the struggles we had, and it all seemed to just flow. Then I cleverly mentioned, "Jason, let me tell Shelly about us being friends. But let's leave out the kiss." Although we both were hurting, it wasn't worth the pain on either side. He agreed and that Saturday we started our official friendship.

After the phone call with Jason, my mom came home with a bunch of shopping bags.

I asked, "Momma, no offense, but how can we afford all these clothes?"

"Well, Woo, your mother has secured a promotion at the office. I thought I would celebrate by splurging a little." I was so excited that I ran over and grabbed the bag like we had won a shopping spree. "Momma, a Mecca dress and new skirts, and knee socks."

"Yes, we deserve this baby." I was so proud of my mom. She told me to change into the outfit and see if it fit. It was an XL. I thought, *man was she trying to tell me I gained some weight.* But it wasn't the time, and she needed my support. We decided to go out to dinner to celebrate her promotion. The only sucky part was Romeo's was right across the street from the school. I would have to see everybody walk into the dance. But I would be fine, I was spending time with my mom and that was precious. We got to the restaurant around 6 and the dance was at 7. So, I could see everyone walk into the dance. I kept glancing over to the school in the middle of the conversation.

My mom finally said, "Woo, why don't you just go to the

dance?"

"Momma, I don't know, it's been hard this last month." I replied feeling sad.

"How? I thought you had good friends and you made the cheerleading squad." Mom gave me that toughen up look.

"I dunno, it seems like I'm just hanging around popular people, but I don't feel that way." "Monica, you listen to me." Fiercely she looked at me. "Who cares what these folks think? Monica, you are smart, beautiful, and a good person." I rolled my eyes.

"Momma you don't understand. You were popular in high school, it's different."

"Ok, it may be different, but you are my child, and you don't run from anything." Mom started aggressively cutting into her steak. "Monica, popularity doesn't mean easy, just be you and have fun." I was chewing my food but listening. "Ok, so I should go to the dance by myself?"

"Monica, sometimes you gotta stand alone to understand what's around you." It was then I knew what to do. My mom saw some co-workers at the restaurant, and I was excused to go across the street to the dance. But my mom reminded me if I ever rolled my eyes at her again I wouldn't have to worry about friends because I wouldn't have a life.

Chapter 11

T hank goodness the dance was casual, and I didn't have to go and change. I had on a red Mecca dress that was right above the knee along with black knee socks and black shoes. I wore my hair down and had a black mini backpack purse as well. At the dance, I ran into the girls over by the photographer getting ready to take a group picture. I came just in time. I walked over and the girls nearly tackled me. Shelly kept complimenting my outfit and Ashley loved my purse. Shelly was wearing a long black velvet dress with a split at the knee and her short hair in nice, neat curls. Ashley decided to wear a red Fubu jersey dress with a black bucket hat and black square heels. Her hair was curly underneath. Jess decided to wear a jean outfit with a white Fila crop top with white K-Swiss. Her hair was all up in a long ponytail with extensions. I could see Jason and Philly staring at us near the punch bowl like we were the Spice Girls or something. We all got in front of the backdrop that was our school colors and took a group friend pose. Yelling "Deuces Up," We all held up our 2 fingers and took a series of silly pictures. After the pic, they all went back to their dates and I hit the dance floor. I was not going to be intimidated by being single. I saw Philly was with a date but being so sweet she let us dance together. Philly and I danced to *"This Is How We Do It"* by Montell Jordan. "Let's do this girl!" "I got you, Philly." Strutting to the dance floor like we were professional dancers from a dance video, we danced, and body rolled and just had a blast. Everyone cheered us on and formed a circle. Our dance skills were on point. People started to clap when we finished. Then the stupid DJ just had to play a slow song. Everyone started to dance with their dates. "*Emotions*" by HTown was playing and I loved that song. I walked over to the restroom to avoid the fact that I didn't have a date. In the bathroom, I fixed one of my loose braids which were all down. Then suddenly I felt a little sad and started to regret coming. Although seeing my friends was cool, I felt like I was only good for kicks and giggles. After I got back from fixing my hair, I sat down and just watched everyone look so happy dancing and looking like they had stars in their eyes. I began to daydream about having a date. But, that dream got interrupted. "BOO!!" I nearly jumped out my chair when Brian screamed in my ear. "Haha, gotcha!" While he was laughing and clapping, I retreated to standard eye rolls.

"Brian, don't you have some fan girl to grope?" I asked while smirking.

"You know you like me rolling up on you, girl." Brian stated as he got closer.

"Where is your usual fan squad?" I asked.

"Oh, I came alone this time, I just wanted to chill, ya know."

"Oh, it must get so exhausting being adored." I was teasing him now as payback. Brian sat down next to me and looked at me with a serious stare.

"Actually, it does." At that moment, Brian seemed normal and real. "You want to dance?" He nudged my shoulder with his hand.

"Sure, I guess."

"Girl what you mean, guess? Come on." He took my hand and led to the middle of the dance floor. Everyone was staring, including Jason. He could tell I was nervous. "Monica?" I was looking down. "Just keep your eyes on me." The song changed to "Kissing You" by Total. Brian had on a Karl Kani all black jogger with that gold hoop earring. As we were dancing, I glanced over at Jess and Mike and they were in a deep conversation. But I didn't care, I was just having fun. Brian even was singing some of the lyrics in my ear. *"I want to kiss you, kissing you is all that I've been dreaming of."* It was so sweet it reminded me of my dance with Jason. Only this was public. As the song wound down, Brian walked me to the curb outside.

"Hey, you wanna hang out tomorrow?" He asked while keeping his hand around my shoulder.

"Alright, cool, just call me. Ashley will give you my number." Brian and I were cool, so it was just hanging out, not a date I said to myself. I had been through hangouts before, so I wasn't going to build this one up into another impossible daydream. He offered me a ride home, but Mr. Jason walked up behind me and with Shelly interjecting himself, "No, Mon, Shelly and I can give you a ride."

"She good bro, I got it." Brian said while staring at Jason while keeping his arm around me.

"Mon, you sure? I mean we don't mind." Jason was now standing in front of me and Brian.

"Jason, it's cool ok? Brian will take care of me." I started while getting a little annoyed.

Then Shelly interrupted, "Jason, she is fine, let's go ok." Jason gave Brian a killer look.

"Yea, alright, let's go, Shel." Brian took me home, but before I got out of the car, he grabbed my hand. "Mon, I want to kiss you."

I said still in shock, "Why?" I began thinking this was a prank or something.

Brian kept talking. "Because I think you cute, ya know... I kind of like you." I was a little suspicious. I had never heard those words before.

"Brian, let's just hang out tomorrow." I agreed.

"Alright, 1 pm."

"Yes, see you then."

He leaned in for a hug and kiss, but I politely shook his hand. I wasn't going to just kiss random boys, my mother raised me better than that. Plus, I had to figure out where this stuff was coming from. Brian had plenty of girls to kiss. He would be fine for the night. Upstairs, in my apartment, I had at least 5 messages blinking. I was too exhausted. I decided to check them tomorrow.

It was rather cold for the end of fall so I put on a purple turtleneck with dark blue jeans and a blue beanie hat to hang out with Brian. My mom helped me toss my braids last night seeing how I wanted a new look. As I was flat ironing my hair, I finally decided to listen to my messages. The first one was from Jess...

Beep...

Hey Mon, it's Jess. Girl, call me I need to talk. I think Mike is... well just call me when you get this.

BEEP...

The next message was from Shelly...

Umm Mon, hey call me girl, I want to talk to you. I think Jason may want to make things official. I don't know. Call me.

Beep

The other 2 were for my mom of people congratulating her on being promoted to Executive Secretary of the law firm. My mom also had earned her paralegal degree last year, so it was perfect timing for her to excel in the law field.

The last one was weird because it was silent for the first few seconds.

Silent breathing ... Hey look um, I need to talk to you about something. Call me.

It was Jason, he probably wanted to talk about Shelly but I wasn't in the mood to discuss anything for him or my crew. I just wanted to focus on hanging out with somebody that really wanted to be my friend and not need anything from me. My mom came in my room to help me with my makeup. "Ok, so Brian, huh?" She was adding liner to my eyes.

"Yea, he just wants to hang out. He is kind of a playa mommy, so I'm just hanging out." My mom really wanted me to wear the fuchsia lipstick, but I kept refusing and wore the dark purple. "Momma can I tell you something?"

"Sure, Woo," Mom was looking confused like I was gonna drop a bomb on her.

"Mom you remember how you wanted me to date Philly?"

"Oh, yes Philly."

"Well momma it kind of hurt my feelings."

"How?" I got up from the chair and sat on the bed.

"It made me feel like I wasn't good enough to have a decent boy that I liked. It just hurt momma." She walked over to me and sat down on the bed.

"Monica Johnson, look at me, you are beautiful, and I didn't mean to hurt you, Woo Woo. It's just Philly seemed like a nice boy and I didn't want you dating guys because of their looks. Sometimes nice guys just need a little help on the outside, but the important part is the inside. I fell for looks with your father and well, you see where it landed us." I finally got it, she didn't want me to get hurt. My dad was a closed subject, but she would speak of him like I knew all the details. We hugged each other tight and I knew she would always have my back no matter what. She finished my makeup and I finished getting ready. I was in the living room when I heard someone at the door. Mom yelled, "Mon, it's Brian."

"Ok, momma, here I come." I walked in holding my black purse like super glue.

"Well look at you, I've never seen you without your braids." "Yes, my hair is pretty thick so braids are just easier."

"Well, I think you should wear it, it's more natural." He was just staring at me.

"Look, Brian make sure you have my daughter back by 10 pm and no funny business. I know the chief of police and the mayor."

"Yes, ma'am." Walking to the car, he opened the door; he had his mom's Jeep. I felt so special for just hanging out. Riding in the car, I noticed Brian was into RnB. He had tapes of Brian McKnight, Toni Braxton and Jodeci. We talked about everything from TV shows to sports. He was surprised how much I liked sports. I was even more delighted that he actually knew every stat known to man. He was highly intelligent.

I asked, "So where are we hanging at today?"

"Oh, it's a surprise." He said.

I hated surprises, but I simply sat back and just rode. "Hey, did you tell Ashley we are hanging out today?"

"I told her; she was cool. Anytime I get away from my parents Ashley nearly pushes me out the door."

"Brian, what's the deal? Why are y'all always arguing?"

He was really open and said, "They just want me to slow down with the ladies, oh and pick a school."

"What are you afraid of?"

"I just want to make the right choice. It's like my parents act like it's their life, you know." I just sat and listened. Brian tried to reach for my hand. But I snatched it away appearing like I was fixing my hair. I didn't want to be all gullible like his groupies. So I just ignored it. It dawned on me he went out with the girls because he felt it was expected of him, but he just wanted someone to talk to. He loved baseball but he wanted his parents to allow him to make more choices. Man, I could be a therapist on *Oprah*.

I cut him off, stressing the point, "Brian, but you haven't been making good ones." He smirked at me. I looked out the window and saw we arrived at some kind of sports gym.

"Um what are we doing, Brian? I put in a heck of a week at cheer and I am tired."

He pouted his lips, "Come on, Monica, please."

"Ok, I guess." I was hoping we didn't have to run because that wasn't my strength at all. We got inside and I saw all of these cages, he really loved baseball. "Brian, I can't play."

"I am gonna teach you." He went over and grabbed a bat and helmet for me to use. But not before clowning my head size I suited up.

I couldn't play but I was highly competitive by nature and didn't like to lose games. At first, I watched him play. He batted really well. I mean any speed the ball came out, he belted them to the back of the facility. Now it was my turn, I didn't want to embarrass myself, so I chose the slowest speed possible. He came up behind me to "show" me how to properly hold a bat. The first pitch came, and I struck out along with the rest of them. I swung around so fast I nearly fell on my butt. Brian couldn't stop laughing.

"What's so funny?"

"You just won't listen."

"Alright, I'm listening"

"You're too worried about what people in here think. Just focus on the pitch and tune out the noise." I did just that. I walked up to the plate and just focused. I squeezed the bat and had a laser eye. The pitch came and I hit the ball. Even though it only went about 10 yards, I still hit the baseball. I was so excited I ran over and gave Brian the biggest hug. We slowly pulled apart and he took off my helmet. "Monica?"

"Yea?" Staring at me like I was a whole snack.

"You ready to go."

"Oh sure, Brian, you just weren't ready for the comeback."

"Girl you need a lot more swings before that could happen." We got back in the Jeep and talked about my technique. We ended up at Miller's for a slice. I didn't really want to go there, but I mean Brian and I were just hanging out, so it was no big deal. I was just his sister's friend whom he flirted with from time to time I kept telling myself. We walked in and everybody was there eating and talking. You would have thought Brian was some kind of king, he was even more popular than Jason.

74

Everybody in Miller's came up to greet him, even people he didn't know. Brian found us a table in a corner, and we sat down, and he ordered a pizza for the table, but I just had a soda. Brian asked, "You not hungry?"

"Not really just thirsty from all that baseball." The girls in Miller's were so bold they walked over to the table and talked to Brian like I wasn't even sitting there. Brian seemed to enjoy all the attention like he was born for the spotlight. He had sunken into that arrogant Brian. He was much cooler alone. But we were just hanging out, so it didn't make a difference. I saw my girls over with their guy friends plus Jason and needed a break from the Brian entourage.

"Hey y'all. How is everyone doing today?"

Jess looked at me and said, "Did you get my message?" "I did, but I have been out today." "Is my brother being nice?"

Raising my eyebrows, "Ashley, we're just hanging out."

"I know, he can be a lot sometimes that's all."

"Yea, it's like rolling with a famous person or something." Jason was just quiet. I almost forgot he was sitting at the table. So much for just being friends.

"Shelly, I got your message too, I'll call you later ok." Shelly kicked me under the table. That meant to shut up about the voicemail. "Ok girl, have fun I guess." Mike and Jess were awkwardly quiet in the corner but I wasn't getting involved.

Brian came up, "Hey Mon, you ready to roll?"

"Yea sure." We got into the jeep and we listened to Brandy's "Broken Hearted".

"Mon, you ever been hurt by a guy?"

"Hmm, I guess. Who hasn't?" I didn't mention it just happened a

75

few weeks ago.

"Well, I would never hurt you, Monica." He glanced over while driving to check my response. I suddenly got flustered and confused. "Why do you think I keep rolling up on you?"

"Um to be annoying." Brian let out a small chuckle. He pulled the car over sharply. You could hear the tires screeching. "Boy, are you trying to kill us both?" Brian turned and looked at me while nervously tugging at his gold earring.

"Monica, I think you're dope as heck." Shocked from the compliment, I pretended to be defensive.

"But what about Ashley?"

"Who do you think thought we would be good together." I was stunned, blinking my eyes fast as light. I just sat back and let the song play out. I didn't understand what was happening. Sitting back up to reconnect.

"Ok, so are you asking me out officially to hang?" Brian grabbed both my hands tightly.

"Girl, what you want me to do, dance?" I chuckled. He opened the car door and turned up the music. Monifah, "I Miss You Come Back Home" was playing. He opened my door and pulled me close to him. Brian placed his hands on my waist, and we grooved. I leaned back with my head on his shoulder.

I was captivated, and without thinking I said, "Brian, yes, I will date you." Riding home I couldn't understand why I said yes so formally. I definitely watched too much TV. But I wasn't daydreaming. This was real and he looked normal. I had a million questions going through my mind.

1. Why does he even like me? I'm Chubby?
2. Was this some weird dare by his friends?
3. Is he just trying to get something from a freshman?
4. How do you have a boyfriend?
5. What would my mother say?
6. I wonder how the girls would react?
7. Would Jason understand?

After the outing with Brian, I went upstairs to my apartment. However, my questions wouldn't go away so I began writing it down into a pro con list.

Pro

Gentleman

Romantic

Sweet

Smart

Like same music

Both love Ashley

Open with feelings

Cons

Graduating this year

College girls

Fan club of groupies

Still had feelings for Jason

Arrogant

Problems w/ parents

I sat in my purple robe and wrote more but I was just scared of what others would say. Chubby girl insecurities arose, but I needed to come out and experience real life. Brian and I could ACTUALLY be a real couple. Not the ones in my head. My freshman year was turning out to be more real life than fiction.

Chapter 12

---◆-◆-◆---

The next week at school was cool because Brian was out of town visiting colleges, so I didn't have to deal with us dating just yet. There were more than enough issues to deal with at Jefferson High. First, Jess and Mike were going through something, Shelly kept wanting my advice about Jason, and whatever else under the sun. I wasn't expecting to see Nikki to walk up to me in the hallway. "Ok, freshman, look, I don't know who you think you are, but I am gonna get my spot back. I didn't work all these years to be snaked out by some fat freshman." I looked at her and couldn't believe what she was saying. I had a flashback of all the jokes, and I snapped. I got all up in her face. She could probably smell my breakfast cereal.

"Look you evil specimen of a human, you got yourself kicked off. So, don't bring your disillusioned self over here because you don't know how to finish what you start." Nikki's eyes got huge and she grabbed my hair. But I didn't flinch, I looked her directly in the eye and said, "Nikki, I highly suggest you let me go, you do not want 10 years of pent-up anger to lash out on that pretty face of yours, do you?" She saw I was serious and let my hair go. She left and went to class, but I knew something else would be coming. Nikki was just too mean at heart. At lunch, I told the crew what happened with Nikki.

Ashley was ready to fight right. Talking superfast, "Where she at?

Who does she think she is…? That crazy wanna-be."

I held my hands up. "Ash slow down, Nikki just talking junk. She just mad about Coach Minnie kicking her off." Ashley started to calm down. The rest of the crew was down for whatever. One thing I could say is our crew didn't tolerate crap even as freshmen. There was so much going on I didn't even tell them about Brian. Jess spoke up, "Ok forget Nikki, what's up with you and Brian?" I was finally ready to share but Mike came over and took Jess to a different table.

"Y'all, what's going on with Jess and Mike?" I asked. "Girl, some girl called her house talking about Mike being with her after he leaves Jess house." Ashley was filling me in on the details. I instantly felt bad for her, but I still didn't want to get involved.

"So, what are we going to do?" Shelly asked.

"Not a thing." I said.

"What do you mean, not a thing?" Shelly questioned.

"Look I tried, and I got my head bit off and was told I didn't understand because I didn't have a boyfriend."

"Wait, what?" Ashley looked confused.

She continued, "Look we need to have a meeting or something because I feel like stuff been going down with everybody and nobody saying nothing." She continued. "Slumber party at my house Saturday night we got some stuff to squash." We all agreed, and Jess would probably come over as well.

After school, the crew all decided to head to the mall as shopping was Ashley's favorite activity. Walking through the mall, we talked about what to do before the sleepover. "I know what we could do, y'all." I spoke up.

"What girl, watch old gymnastics videos?" Ashley said with a chuckle.

"Hardy, ha ha." Shelly replied with a grin.

"Come on, Monica, just say it." Ashley had little patience. "Y'all, a haunted house." All the girls stopped and looked at me like it was the best idea ever. We stopped at the food court to discuss the matter.

"A haunted house?" Jess questioned. "Just us girls, no boys?" Ash asked, looking confused again. "I didn't say that y'all." I replied. It looked to me like even entertaining just girls was not going to fly with this crew. Shelly began staring at us with a smirk.

So, I stated, "I'm kind of tired of the double dates." I said annoyed.

"Not a date, just a group outing, we could invite some of the guys and even some of the cheer team." Shelly suggested. My eyebrows were raised. We all looked at each other slightly excited, grabbing hands tightly. "So, we are going to a haunted house Saturday?" Everyone looked at each other. "Yes," We all said in unison. Our next stop was to find a cute outfit. I had just gotten my allowance and I wanted to get these black jeans and this cute off the shoulder mustard fitted shirt with a huge black belt to hide my lil pooch tummy. Thank goodness it was on sale and they had my size. With my working out with cheer I was down to a size 14 so I could shop on the lower end of the plus section. I could even squeeze into a 12 if it was stretchy, which meant I could shop with my friends in their stores. We spent the rest of time looking for an outfit for Jess to wear to the OutKast concert in a few weeks. When I got home, I was beat. My mom was in one of her moods and was cooking everything in the free world.

"Hey baby, did you find what you were looking for."

"Yes, ma'am." I went into my room to take off my shoes and get ready for the shower.

"MONICA!" My mom called.

"MA'AM!"

"There is a message for you on the phone."

"Alright momma, can I check it when I get out of the shower?"

"No, you might wanna listen now." She had walked over to my bedroom doorway at this point. "Alright, momma I'm coming." I wondered if it was Brian because he hadn't called since our date. I wasn't tripping if he didn't call. I wouldn't be bothered with more drama. I pushed the button... Beep

Hey, Roni, it's me. Look I am gonna be in town Saturday and I want to see if I can see you all. I will be at the Radisson, alright? Please call me.

I looked at my mom confused. "Who was that momma, some dude?" I laughed. She didn't respond and looked at me and told me to sit down. Our dining room table was next to the kitchen. "Monica, that was your dad." My stomach started doing literal flips.

"My dad?"

"Yes, it's him." Momma said. All I knew is that his name was Jeffery Johnson, I only knew that because I found some old papers in my mom's dresser.

"Sooo...are we gonna see him?" My mom just sat there rubbing her hands together. I asked again. "Momma why don't we talk about him?" All of my life I never asked out of respect for my mom because it was just us and my aunts. I knew he was alive, but my mom just kept it private. "Mom, I kind of want to meet him."

"I know baby...It's just so much I have been trying to protect you from." I could tell this was hard for my mother. She had worked hard for us to live in this town and make it as an executive.

So, I said it for her. "Momma I don't have to see him, ok." I gave her a long hug and went to the shower. Although I knew she wanted to tell me something, I left it alone, for now.

Chapter 13

The week flew by in a breeze. I sat in the cafeteria with the crew as we discussed what snacks we wanted for the slumber party. We also had our group set for the haunted house at the field. It would be Jason, Philly, Eric, Melody, and a few upperclassmen. It seemed like it would be fun. Leaving for the day, I ran smack into Brian and his entourage. "Miss Monica, my favorite freshman." He was acting brand new. I thought, *not another guy who is embarrassed by me*. Before I knew it, he pulled me up to his 6 ft plus frame and gave me the biggest hug and a lingering kiss on the cheek. My cheeks turned blush. Holding on to me he whispered in my ear, "Let's talk later." Brian had a serious look on his face. "Ok," I said. He let go of my waist to continue the conversation. "I'll call you later tonight, ok?" The entourage didn't seem to care, and they actually spoke to me. Walking out of the cafeteria I felt like I could see Brian actually being more than a friend. But the "talk" had me nervous. Only time would tell as I had zero experience in the romance department.

Before we left, we had cheer practice. I never realized cheerleading could be so tough, the constant moving and lifting. Not every girl was as fresh as they needed to be. Which could be awkward when you have someone's feet on your shoulder. Although I had improved, I was far off from being an MVP. It appeared as though the girls were getting frustrated with my novice level.

"Mon, you have to get tighter if you're gonna be on this team."

"Yea, girl come on." Another cheerleader spoke up. The team was riding me, but I was willing to take it. I had been exposed to cheer life and I wasn't turning back. Before cheer practice ended, Coach wanted to try the stunt again. I was so nervous because I was holding the top flyer. She called the stunt. "Up, 1234." Melody was up right on my shoulders. "I'm slipping." Melody yelled. Instead of panicking like I had in the past, I grabbed her ankles and told her, "I GOT YOU...STAY TIGHT!" She adjusted and we stuck the stunt. We ran it like 5 more times perfectly. After that last stunt, they all tackled me for getting better. It felt so good, I started enjoying cheer as a sport and not for popularity. I guess hard work pays off.

Saturday couldn't come quicker for me, I had this feeling that it would be a great weekend.

That morning I was listening to my mom's Anita Baker tapes. Caught up in the rapture of love.

I couldn't stop thinking about falling in love. What it would be like? I enjoyed watching *Coming to America* and wondered if I would meet some prince. Or would I meet a bad boy that needed to be loved by a good girl. The lyrics swayed through my head while I was cleaning my room. *Ah, caught up in the rapture of love. Nothing else can compare. When I feel the magic of you. The feeling is always new.* Then I got my bathrobe on to head to the showers. I had my mother's strawberry and champagne Victoria's Secret body wash, spray, and powder to have the perfect scent. Hanging out reminded me of just feeling good. I took the radio into the bathroom so I could hear some more music. Then, "Brandy" came on...*I wanna be down, with what you're going through... I wanna be down with you...* Oh I just couldn't wait for this to happen to me. Somehow it seemed that in a couple of months, I went from bad fashion to decent. And 1 friend to 4 tight friendships. No boyfriend to having a kiss of confusion and a real date. But hey, I wasn't counting. After I slapped on my splash spray, I put on the outfit I bought at the mall. I had the mustard shirt on, and I tucked my bra straps to the side so my shoulders could be seen. I had built a little muscle and I mean little from being a cheer manager and joining the team. But that chubby belly was poking. Thank goodness I had my big belt buckle to hide the bulge. Putting on the belt, I was attempting to buckle the front. I gave it a good tug and the belt snapped. I threw up my hands and flopped on my bed, nearly bouncing off. I had the perfect outfit, and I couldn't wear it now. "MOMMMM!"

"What's wrong!" My mom screamed running into my bedroom.

"Mommy, my belt." I sounded like a straight up baby. "Mom what am I going to wear now...this really sucks...This haunted house will be with the crew and some of the upper-class girls."

"Monica, why do you care about this little belly of yours? You look great, baby." She said, squeezing my thigh. I just sat there and thought about the jokes. Middle school was calling my name. My mom still didn't understand what I was going through because she never experienced being constantly bullied by people. It was too late to change clothes, so I had to think quickly. I found a thinner belt to wear and I could just cover my belly when all else failed. I took my hair down from my scarf and brushed it out. I had a mustard beanie hat to match my shirt. I wasn't a big makeup person but for tonight I threw on some eyeliner.

Nearly poking my eye out, I slowed down to put it on. I wore some clear lip gloss, so my lips didn't look like a crack in the sidewalk. I had to hurry because Ashley's mom would be here soon. I ran down the stairs out of my apartment nearly breaking my neck. "Come on, girl, everyone is waiting!" Ashley was yelling, waving me to hurry. I got to the car and the front was empty. I sat down and Brian was in the driver's seat. "Um ok, Brian what are you doing? I thought your mom was driving." "Well, I decided to drive and hang out, since Ashley told me about it, I thought it would be fun." I rolled my eyes. I hadn't forgotten that he didn't call me later that day. Ashley and Shelly were in the back seat and laughing at Brian's comments. I don't know why I felt nervous. Brian looked great with his long sleeve blue and white striped Polo shirt and dark jeans. I glanced down and he had the new Timberland's on his feet. I turned on the radio station. Brian gently smacked my hand. "Hey, you don't touch a man's stereo. I got a tape already, Mon." I just huffed a little and started talking about his mixtape. I turned around in my seat to talk to the girls since Brian was tripping over his stereo.

"So, you guys ready for this haunted house?" Ashley was holding Shelly's hand already. "I'm ready but Shelly over here is scared." Shelly looked petrified.

"Hey, in South Carolina we don't play with stuff like that." "Stuff like what?" I asked. "Spirits and stuff…that stuff ain't right y'all." Shelly was looking out the window like it was a monster outside. Sometimes I forgot about Shelly's southern accent. I guess I got used to it. We all started laughing hard. Catching my breath, "Shelly, it's just like a haunted house from the movies….fake…you gone be alright." I turned back around to jam to "Steelo" by 702. "Brian this playlist is dope." The window was cracked, it had gotten chilly. I was glad I brought my jean jacket. We pulled up to the haunted house. Everyone was already waiting in line. Jess and the rest waved us down to get in the line. "Brian you actually gonna hang with us?" I asked, bumping my shoulder into his chest. While observing his fan club over in the parking lot.

"Yeah, I am. Even though somebody didn't ask me?" I crossed my arms and looked right at him. He was about an inch and half taller than me.

"Well, if someone had called me earlier, maybe you would have known."

Brian just shook his head and said, "Girl come on." He grabbed my hand and interlocked his fingers into mine. My heart was jumping, but I had to remain calm. Ashley and Shelly were grinning ear to ear. I decided to grab some hot apple cider before going into the line. Brian grabbed some for Jess too. We walked over to the line hand in hand. Everyone from our school was looking at us like foreign aliens. I started to get scared. He was the most sought-after guy in the school and he was holding my hand. Usually, when you're that girl, everyone hates you and dogs you daily. What would I say to people? We hadn't clarified our relationship and had one date. I started to let go of his hand, but he just grabbed it tighter. He leaned over to me and whispered, "It's gonna be ok." I just decided to go with the flow. I got to the line and the guys started arguing about random sports topics. Jason and Shelly started talking to each other. Philly was trying to talk to Melody. But apparently Melody didn't seem to notice him. In fact, she was checking her watch while he was trying to talk. We got to the door and Brian stood behind me holding my hips. But at a distance. He knew not to play with me.

The haunted house was pretty scary. I literally had my nails in Brian's arm while random screaming at Freddie Krugers and ghosts were jumping out. Grabbing Brian's shirt, I placed my head in his chest.

"BRIAN...BRIAN... Something just touched me. I wanna go...OH MY Lord get me out." Brian was a gentleman and let me keep my head there.

"Babe just hold on, it's almost over." I said, nearly tripping in the grass.

"Brian, you better not be playing, I am DONE!!" Something started chasing us with a chainsaw. I ran so fast you could see the smoke from my feet. I even forgot Brian was still towards the back. I hunched over and placed my hands on my knees to catch my breath. Finally, we were out. Brian thought it was funny and Shelly left at the halfway point; she couldn't take it. Philly left with her. They were both chickens. Afterwards we all stood near the exit and laughed about Shelly and Philly leaving early.

"Man, I don't care what y'all fools say. That mess was scary." Philly stated loudly. I leaned onto Brian, laughing on his chest.

"So, let's roll out to Miller's and get a slice. I'm hungrier than a mug." Jason suggested. He was being rather calm.

"Nope, we are having a girl's night." Shelly proudly stated.

"Nope, we coming too." Philly said placing his hand on the small of my back. Brian shot him a look and he moved his hand. "Bye, guys, see y'all at school Monday." I noticed that Jason didn't hug Shelly goodbye. Mike drove Jess over to Ashley's and we got back in the car with Brian. When we got to Ashley's her mom had ordered pizza for us and had all our favorite snacks. I loved their mom. Brian ate with us.

"Soo... are y'all a couple or what?" Jess asked bluntly. I nearly choked on my popcorn.

"That's my business." Brian said while having a slight smile. "Any who7, what y'all think about Philly getting all scared and stuff." I changed the subject. They knew I didn't feel comfortable talking about it. Brian's mom came into the den area where we eating to tell Brian it was time for him to depart.

"Bye, Brian," All the girls said in unison. After we ate, dinner we all went upstairs to shower and put on pjs. Now that I was kind of kickin' it with Brian, I had to make sure I looked halfway decent. I reached in my purple overnight bag and grabbed my cheer t-shirt and a pair of blue shorts. On the way to Ashley's room I had to pass Brian's. I peeked my head around his door frame to see he was actually studying. Brian was laying sideways on his bed with a white sleeveless t-shirt on with gray sweats. I didn't realize how huge his arms were. My goodness. I was staring so hard I tripped over something on the floor. Brian looked up and chuckled. "You want to come in?" His eyebrows raised and gesturing for me to come inside.

"Brian, no yo momma gonna think I'm fast...I'm cool." Brian got off the bed to walk towards me.

"Girl, I just wanna show you my room." He was standing now in the doorway looking into my eyes.

"No, really, Brian, I'll see in the morning." Brian started backing up.

"Alright, Miss Monica." I shook my head and walked into Ashley's room. We were all waiting for Jess to get off the phone with Mike; they were in the middle of another argument. I was getting tired of them arguing all the time. Jess hung up the phone and looked puzzled as to why we all were staring at her.

"Jess what's going on with you and Mike, girl." Shelly asked.

"Oh noooo...you can't ask her those questions, right Jess?" Jess looked over at me confused. "Remember the letter?" Ashley glanced over at me. "What letter?" Ashley asked.

"Well, Jess sort of wrote a letter talking about not interfering in their darn relationship and that I couldn't understand because I didn't have a boyfriend."

"Yeah and?" Jess asked. I wanted to punch Jess in the face.

"Well... that junk hurt, Jess." I said looking frustrated. "It made me feel like I wasn't important and that I wouldn't ever fit in...You know how rough middle school was for me." Jess stood up raising her arms.

"Yea and I never teased you." She sat back down.

"I know you didn't, but it made me feel like I was right back in 7th and 8th grade."

"How Mon?"

"If you haven't noticed I'm not the slimmest Jess, and…" I started to get choked up. "You guys are all like freakin' models and can wear whatever you like." I was venting now. "I mean you even wanted me to go out with Philly, not a quality guy. Why? Because that's all that would date me…Sometimes y'all make me feel like the outsider." My eyes were slowly watering. I walked over to sit on Ashley's bed and grab a pink pillow. "It's hard every time we go out it feels like I'm just the fat friend along for the ride."

"That's not true, Mon." Shelly stood up and stuck her foot out and folded her arms.

"You were just out tonight with a guy so how are you any different." I stood up and looked at Shelly. She was right, Brian was showing me interest. But I still felt suspect about his intentions.

"Mon, I never thought of you like that. I mean you're so courageous and beautiful." It wasn't normal to hear those words from friends. It sounded like a foreign language to me. "Everyone would die for your hair and that skin, my goodness." I lifted my head and gave them a smile to show them the situation was resolved. But I was lying to them. I wanted to tell them, even though Brian liked me, I really didn't believe it. That pushing Philly on me made me feel like I wasn't worth it to have a guy like Brian. The fact that they never asked me who I liked. It was like they assumed I was content with just being their friend., but I didn't. I was just too scared and decided to keep my truth inside.

"Girl, you gotta tell us when you feel like that. We are your girls." Ashley said like a true friend. Everyone began looking at Jess. She took a deep breath before speaking.

"I guess it's my turn now."

"Jess, you don't have too." Shelly said. We all were emotionally tired. But Jess kept talking.

"As far as Mike goes, I was just embarrassed. I know y'all hear the rumors about him cheating." She ran off a list of girls that Mike had been accused of being with. Jess was just hurt. She was even contemplating losing her virginity to him.

"Jess, I say forget him, girl, he is too much drama." I said standing over her like a concerned mother.

"Have you caught him?" Shelly asked.

"No, I haven't. Just rumors." Jess replied.

"As your friend Jess, something feels off and I want you to be careful, girl. Remember your body is sacred, don't let anybody have it all willy nilly." Jess understood, but we all knew she wasn't done with him just yet. I didn't have the courage to tell the girls about Jason and our random encounters. I figured since Jason was so embarrassed by me it wasn't worth discussing.

"Shelly, what happened with Jason, and why was he acting so weird tonight?" Ashley asked. Shelly was sitting on the floor with legs crossed looking hurt.

"I mean I guess he just needs some time, with football and school. He just wants to be cool for a while." All of us looked at each other.

"Do you think he has a girlfriend?" Jess asked.

"I don't think so, but hey I can wait... Right?" Shelly was waiting for approval.

"Of course you can wait, Shel, Jason is a good guy, but while you wait there's nothing wrong with exploring options. Remember you're Jeffersonville's southern belle." Shelly was smiling ear to ear. Our crew went a little deeper tonight. We discussed things that we would hold to the vest for life.

Winter

Chapter 14

---◆—◆—◆---

The holidays went by so fast it seemed like we didn't even have a break. I spent 2 weeks at my grandmother's house along with my other cousins. My family happens to be full of loudmouth women. The men in our family just kind of sat around, watched sports, barbecued, and took out trash. They always conveniently stood in the garage to avoid whatever topic was being discussed by the women. My grandparents were local business owners of a couple grocery stores. Grandmother is what Josephine Clark wanted her grandchildren to call her. She once said that "grandma" was a name for people that had no manners. Ironically, people said I favored grandmother. She had almond shaped eyes with a honey caramel complexion. She wore her dark brown hair down with bouncy curls that ran down to the middle of her back. Every time gray hair appeared, there was a convenient trip to the beauty parlor. My grandfather was tall and wore his head bald. He had the shape of an offensive lineman with a wide chest and big shoulders. Grandpa was super chill as he was used to the antics of the women in this family. Everyone in Alberta, IN knew who they were. Heck, even a few people knew them in other parts of the state. I often wondered how my relatives had so much money, but we were barely getting by. The family had their usual conversations about how my mom should have gone to a four-year college and how come she let me get so chubby. My family was the type that didn't care what was said. And they couldn't give a crap if your feelings were hurt. But I was used to them at this point. My cousins were all smarty pants with too much money. My aunts were lawyers and my uncles worked in the corporate world, but had blue collar values. My aunts made sibling rivalry look like a piece of cake compared to their courtroom style debates. The sister arguments were legendary, but I had no energy to discuss why everything from tripping on the sidewalk to rude waitresses apparently was a lawsuit. My Aunt Diana was the middle child and a bankruptcy lawyer. She was always talking to me about saving money. She was about the same size as my mom, fair skinned. She always wore a short Halle Berry cut. Aunt Diana always said it was too hot to have any amount of hair on her neck. Aunt Melissa was the oldest, but she was kind of a free spirit by nature, but she was no punk. She wore hair extensions, so I didn't actually know what type of hair she had. Aunt Melissa has a mocha complexion and about 5'9" inches tall. She worked as a tax lawyer but had since decided to stay home and raise my cousins. She was slightly taller than my mom and a little darker. I would always tell people don't let her niceness fool you. She was known to beat down anybody in the town of Alberta. Once my mom told me grandmother sent her to finishing school to address her tomboy antics. I thought it was funny because Aunt Melissa definitely still would throw down if needed. Momma and my aunts were close and were always on the phone. They were always sending her on dates trying to get her a man.

But my mom was trying to make money and get us into a home. She had me at the age of 18, right out of high school. We lived with my grandmother for a couple years until she got a job in Jackson. She also enrolled in college right when I finished 5th grade. Jackson was only about an hour away from Alberta, so we went to my grandmother's for Sunday dinners at least twice a month. I once asked my mom why we didn't just stay with grandmother until she finished her degree. She told me that always have your own and never depend on nobody for a handout. Years later, it still rang true. She motivated me to do the best I can in school and always try my best. The only thing was my mom worked so much she barely had time for my activities or for my so needed fashion advice. It wasn't her fault, though. She was trying her best and since I started high school she had gotten better with listening to me. She still didn't have time to come to any of my cheer activities. Yet it was just us together until the wheels fly off. The fam was all in the kitchen talking about Aunt Melissa's many fights as a child when I got called into the backroom by grandmother. The hallway to my grandmothers room had pictures dating back to the late 1800's of successful Clark's. Her room was fitting for a royal queen. Grandmother had satin gold blankets and pillows. French Antiques flowed all over her room, us kids knew not to touch them. I knocked gently, "Grandmother, can I enter?" "Yes, Monica come have a seat." I sat in her white rocking chair. "Your mother tells me that you are doing better in school and you made the cheer team." She was sitting in a rocking chair. "Monica, have you tried the diet I told you about?"

"Yes ma'am, but I really don't eat much, it's just my stomach." I said, feeling uncomfortable.

"Well, look you can do it, you're a Clark. Even your grandmother struggled with her weight once. These years are precious, I know you want a boyfriend, right?"

"Sort of," I said, hunching my shoulders.

"Look Monica, you are so pretty I hate to see you not enjoy high school because of this pesky weight. If you need my help, just call me, your mother acts like it doesn't exist."

"Yes, ma'am" I left the room feeling sorry for myself that I had not lost this weight. Almost like I let the family down. None of my cousins were heavy at all. They were all popular at their schools and had boyfriends. At every family function my cousins would talk about their boyfriends. I never had anything to share. This time I did, but when I brought up Brian who, was known statewide, they were looking at each other as if I weren't telling the truth. My cousin asked, "So, Brian huh?" I just sat quiet I couldn't blame them. In the past, I might have made up a couple boyfriends just to fit in only to be flat busted. One time I said the reason I couldn't call my boyfriend was because his phone had got cut off but then the next day slipped up and said we spoke the previous night. What did they expect me to do? I loved my cousins, but it's kind of hard to jump in some conversations when you know how bad your love life stunk. Looking down at my watch, I was so ready to go. I sat tapping my feet looking out the window and I saw my uncles on the back patio barbecuing. My uncles would barbecue any time of day or season which made getting thin a problem in my department. I enjoyed watching them growing up because they were chill, and I didn't have to discuss my weight. But they never failed me when they would argue about how to arrange the coals on the grill. My Uncle Bert was my Aunt Melissa's husband. He was about 5'10" with a little beer belly. He also had a dark brown complexion with a mini afro. Uncle Earl was super tall and even brighter than Aunt Diane and was really skinny. He had a bald head with a small beard on his face. The way they argued, you wouldn't know they worked for anybody's corporation.

I went outside just when they were mixing the coals. "Bert, you are doing it all wrong. You need to spread out these coals. Stacking them won't keep the grill going." Uncle Earl was standing next to Uncle Bert bundled up in a black puffy winter coat.

"Earl, I am telling you, stacking them will heat the whole dogon grill." Uncle Bert kept moving the coal around with a stick, frustrated that it wasn't heating up fast. As cold as it was, I walked over to them laughing.

"What's going on out here? Y'all are mad funny." Uncle Earl put his hand around my shoulder to give me a quick side hug.

"Well, your Uncle Bert here has a wish to give the whole family salmonella when the meat is not cooked right." Uncle Earl let out a side chuckle. Uncle Bert threw his hands in the air.

"Earl, you don't know what you're talking about because your barbecue is always dry." Uncle Earl stopped his chuckle and pointed his finger at Uncle Bert.

"Now that's it, Bert. My barbecue is just fine, and you would know that if Melissa ever let you out the house." They continued bickering for the next hour until they agreed to stack the coals like Uncle Bert wanted in the beginning. I was happy when momma said it was time to leave. I hugged all my fam and told them goodbye. By the time we made it home from Alberta we were exhausted. Busting through the door, I bolted to my room, put on my plush purple robe and flopped on my bed. Momma was tired too, we had enough of the family for the evening. I was thinking I only had 2 more days before school started for the second semester. Jeffersonville had entered winter and it was colder than snowy this year with an exception for Christmas Eve. Throughout town we had plenty of lights down through town square. It was tradition to not remove the lights until Valentine's Day. Jeffersonville had a myth that only love could dim lights. Before heading to Alberta, I spent a little time with Brian. After the sleepover he took me on a couple of dates. The first date was to the movies, guessing he wanted to prove he could be quiet during a film. The second date was at this really cool burger joint with classic films all over the walls. We actually had a great time. Good conversation and plenty of laughs. Brian was always a gentleman and calm, but we hadn't had a chance to discuss if we were official. He kept saying over break that he wanted to "talk". But I never got the chance and now that I was home, I planned to avoid him. Anytime people wanted to talk it was never good. Every soap opera known to man knew that. I remember one soap where the girl was so into the guy and it turned out he just needed a friend to get through a rough spot. I didn't want to find out either. Sitting on my bed, I saw a little present with a yellow bow on my dresser. I got up quickly and yelled "MOM, is this mine!"

"OHHH, yes I forgot to give you that gift." Ripping the gift apart like a 5-year-old was a tactic I couldn't seem to rid myself of as of yet. It was another journal with a note inside.

> *My beautiful daughter,*
>
> *Here is another journal for you. I noticed you were almost writing at the end of your other one. I know I have been working a lot in the past but with this new job I get off by 4 pm and I plan to be at your next game. And*

help you with any cheers if you need me. Use this journal to write your thoughts and don't forget to use me when you really need to talk. Don't doubt yourself, baby, you are going to be just fine. Trust me. Oh, and don't live your life to satisfy others. I pray you enjoy this journal, baby.

Merry Christmas,

Your mother

Chapter 15

This gift was better than anything I got including a gift card to a number of plus size clothing stores, a CD Walkman, a pair of tennis shoes, and a bunch of smell goods. I had decided to roller set my hair and wear it curly for school on Monday. I had all the foam lotion and the rods to make it look the bomb. The only thing no one told me is that running a hair dryer over your hair in the morning before school would keep them dry. My hair looked like wet noodles. My mom had left for work already, so I just grabbed a claw clip and some gel and slicked it back into the clip. Since my hair was a mess, I didn't wear my new long jean dress I got over the holiday. So, I wore a black Mecca t-shirt with my blue jean overalls. At my locker, the crew was back, and they looked great. They all had their new clothes on ready for '97. Ashley had on a long navy-blue crushed velvet dress with her signature curls. She also had a pink mini backpack with black stack shoes. Shelly slipped into a fuzzy red sweater with black slacks. Jess rounded it off with a black fitted blazer and a mid-thigh skirt. I don't know how she got this one passed the dress code. "Mon, what happened to the denim dress, and the rods." Shelly was fiddling through my hair.

"Um, nobody told me that you had do them at night." They started cracking up.

"Whatever, there's always tomorrow, ladies."

"Speaking of tomorrow, Brian says y'all are supposed to hang out." Ashley said with a huge grin.

"Girl, I don't know I think he is trying to dismiss me in a nice way."

"Why you say that? I mean all he told me at after breakfast was that y'all had plans."

"Did he say anything about having a talk with me?"

"Girl I don't get involved, you're my homegirl and he is my brother and that's it. I left y'all situation alone after I said it was cool y'all could hang."

"Man, Ash, I really think he is gonna end our kicking it, I mean he graduates this year and we never clarified our friendship. Huhhhh, why does this stuff have to be so hard." The girls looked at me.

"It's only hard if you make it that way." Jess said with confidence. "I can't figure out why he likes me, y'all." Ash stopped and looked me in the eyes.

"Because you're a nice person inside and out."

"Thanks Ash."

"Come on...you my girl, just see what he says." We all left for class. With a new semester I had advanced English and it was with the worst teacher in the free world. Mrs. Roby had a reputation for giving an obscene amount of homework on Fridays and only passing half the class, if that. I didn't want to be a writer or anything, but there was something about English class that always piqued my curiosity. The only sucky part was none of my home-girls were in this class, just a few freshman and sophomores who were placed there because of the 10th grade English class being full. Advanced English was like taking 10th grade English. I was writing down the assignment in my notebook and somebody was asking me for a pencil. I hated when people did that, I mean, come prepared. But it was Jason, so I let it go. After class, he walked me to my locker to put up my book and get my other things for my next class.

"So how was your break?"

"It was cool just hanging out with family, you know." We kept walking.

"So, you wanna study later at the library? This first assignment looks crazy hard."

"How about Friday, it's not due for a week plus I have cheer practice." Jason's season was over, but we still had to cheer for the basketball team. The bell rang and we went our separate ways. I could still smell the Zest soap and it drove me crazy. But Jason still didn't like me enough to confront his friends. Even with me "dating" one of the most popular seniors in the school, Jason still saw me as the chubby friend. The next couple of days were busy, between adjusting to a new semester and cheer it was hard to even think about my personal life. I had been ignoring Brian's phone calls and avoiding him at school. I don't think I could take being dumped or sidelined. It was just easier to pretend our dates didn't exist. Before I knew it, Friday was here, and I was rushing to meet Jason at the library since we didn't have cheer practice. I sat at the library and waited about 20 minutes and still no Jason. My thoughts began to go crazy. I knew he couldn't see me as a girlfriend but studying, come on, man. "I'm so sorry, Mon." I looked up at him.

"What the heck, Jason, you asked me for help... I do have a life."

He sat down and whispered. "Mon, we are in a library."

"Why are you late Jason?"

"I got up with the guys and things ran over, I am so sorry…" He pouted his silly lips out. Why couldn't I resist him still. "You got your things, boy?"

"Yes, I do MA'AM!" After we cleared things up, we started studying, but with the two of us we got done pretty quick, I guess great minds think alike. "Well, Mon, I hear you're trying out for the play."

"Yep, you're right. I am so excited!"

"I'm sure you'll get the part."

"Why do you say that?"

"Because once you put your mind to something, Mon, you always pull through… I mean look at you. You're a cheerleader now because you worked hard not by just standing around waiting but with hard work." I smiled and so did Jason. We continued to talk about everything and laughed so much we almost got kicked out of the library. I was grabbing my books and Jason asked to meet again next week. I told him that was fine, but it had to be Saturday around 11 am because games were on Friday's this season. Then all of a sudden Jason got quiet and was looking behind me.

Whispering I said, "Jason…. Jason, what's wrong?" I turned around and I saw Brian walking lighting fast to our table.

"Babe… you can't call me or return my calls, huh, Monica?" My eyes were as large as a cow.

"Brian, what are YOU doing here?"

"No, Monica, what are you doing here?"

"Look, get your books and let's go." He grabbed my book-bag.

Jason hadn't dropped his glance off Brian.

"Hey look, Mon, you gone be alright?" Brian looked at Jason squinting his eyes.

"Bro, look, this don't have nothing to do with you, so chill man." Jason stood up looking defensive, his eyes still on Brian.

"Like I said, you good, Mon?" They were now standing eye to eye. I had never seen this side of Jason. Brian was Mr. It and nobody challenged him PERIOD. I grabbed Jason's arm.

"I'm good, Jason, just go home ok." He looked over at me.

"You sure?"

"Yea, I'm sure." Jason got his things and left. I turned my eyes to Brian.

"Your car, NOW!" The people in the library didn't know whether to call the police or help me. I got into the car and slammed the door. "Look, let's get one thing straight. As long as you black, don't you ever clown me like that again in public."

"Monica you not answering my calls or nothing, what's up… I told you I needed to talk to you."

"Brian, let's not gloss over you acting like a complete idiot just now." He took a couple deep breaths calming down slowly.

"Monica…look I need to talk with you about some things. Please, just listen to me. He sounded serious. Maybe I had misread the "talk."

"Ok, Brian I'm listening." Brian turned towards me in his seat.

"I decided to go and play for Arizona State." I sat silent. I knew this was it, he was traveling far away and now he wanted to end things. So I acted overly happy.

"Wow, that's great Brian, when did you decide?"

"Over break after my visit. Only thing is I would have to leave 2 days after graduation."

"Wow, that's pretty fast…are you ready for that? What about your family?"

"They know, it's all good. I am still not 100 percent but it's what my family says will fast track me to the pros after a year."

"So that's what you wanted to talk about." I took my hand and smacked my forehead for thinking it was something else.

"Yea, sort off."

"Ok spit it out Brian, I have to get home."

"Monica, I never met a girl like you… I mean you're not all up my butt or trying to just hang around because of baseball. You just like me for me."

"So, what are you saying to me Brian."

"I want you to be my girl." I just looked at him nearly crying. I had never been asked that question ever. It felt good, but my chubby issues were at the front of my brain. "Brian, I meant to ask you this, how do you feel about my…size?"

"What about it?"

"I mean I'm not the smallest girl, Brian."

"Monica, you act like you're 400 pounds. You just got some curves and I love it." Curves he told me, I just called it fat. "Monica, you're beautiful, and I want us to explore a deeper connection… And again, I'm sorry for going a little loco on you tonight. I'm just not used to being ignored."

"Brian, I will try and do better ok. But if this is going to work, we have to respect and trust each other." Brian pulled me closer to him, kissing my forehead.

"I will always respect you baby."

"Ok, boyfriend." I looked up at him and we just held each other. "OHHH, by the way, psycho, who told you where I was?" He looked down at me while we were still hugging.

"Your mom." I thought when I got home me and mom had to discuss girl code. Riding in the car, Brian walked me to the door and told me he would pick me up Monday for school but to be ready for the celebration dinner Sunday night.

"Brian, I don't know. What should I wear?"

"Don't worry it's dressy casual."

"What time is the dinner?"

"I'll come get you around 8. Is that cool?"

"Yea, sure." I went into the door because I didn't know how to say goodbye. Brian pulled me back and gave me a sweet kiss on the cheek.

"Goodnight, girlfriend." My eyes lit up.

"Goodnight, boyfriend." My mom was in bed reading this new book everyone was raving about called *Waiting to Exhale*. I walked in her room to talk about her ratting me out and about my new relationship. "Mommy, I have a boyfriend." Looking up from her book mommy patted on the bed for me to sit next to her.

"Woo, I know this means so much to you, and I am happy for you, but make sure to be careful." I knew what careful meant. "Remember, your body is sacred and if a man can't treat you like the queen that you are then you DON'T need them." I looked at my mom.

"I will, mommy." She hugged me like I was a little girl again, tight and with extra warmth.

"OH, shoot...Monica, please call that boy." "Ma, I already talked to Brian. Thanks for telling him where I was at."

"Girl, please, I don't care, I'm talking about Jason. He has called here a million times. I thought y'all just were friends. What's going on?"

"Nothing, ma." I was emotionally exhausted. I flopped down in my bed and pulled the covers up and debated on whether I should call Jason. I was officially with Brian now, but Jason was my friend. I decided to call Jess and the girls to tell them what happened first. But I called Jason to tell him I was fine, and I would see him at school.

Chapter 16

———————◆—◆—◆———————

Sunday after church was great, I really felt connected and so did my mom. She was thankful for how God continued to bless us. At the house, we decided not to drive up to Alberta to see grandmother but go to a local soul food restaurant. My mom was making good money now and she really wanted to spend a little bit of it just to see what it felt like. But I still had my dad on my mind; ever since he left that voicemail, it was hard to shake it. As we sat down for lunch, I felt this urge to ask her a lot of questions. "Mommy, I want to ask you something, but you have to promise not to get upset." My mom paused, using her fork to poke around at her greens. She looked uncomfortable but I wasn't going to let it go. "Mom, what happened between you and my dad?" She just kept poking at her food and ignoring my question. I leaned in towards her saying, "Mommy, look if you don't want to talk about it fine. But I have a right to know." I never met the man and survived on TV dads to know what one was like, so I never discussed it. But now I just needed to know.

"Look, your dad is a really hard topic for me." I maintained eye contact.

"But why, mom?" Trying to sound very mature. "I will say this, Monica, I really loved your dad and he really loved you." I could see the pain in my mom's eyes, her eyes were welling and it looked like she even struggled to breathe. I grabbed my mom's hand and squeezed it tight as she couldn't even look me in the eyes. It was then I knew that whatever was going on with my dad I would have to find on my own. It was just too painful for my mom. "Mommy its cool." I meant just that, I was done asking, the next time she would have to come to me. The rest of the afternoon I spent getting ready for Brian's celebration dinner. I called Ashley but she didn't answer the phone. I hung up my cordless phone and then called Jess but no answer. My last call would have been to Shelly, but her family was probably still having Sunday brunch. So, I called someone that I thought could help me in a crunch.

"Hey, I need your help." I said in a panicky voice.

"Monica, what's wrong?"

"You've been on dates, right?"

"Um, yea."

"What do you wear to like a family dinner type thing? I mean, I have a church outfit, or maybe like jeans and a cute shirt, or like a really nice dress." I was rambling.

"Monica, calm down, and where is the place?" Jason asked sounding groggy, like I woke him up.

"I don't know, Brian didn't tell me."

"Ok, look this isn't my specialty but I would wear something churchy. That way you're not overdressed and not too casual, you know?"

"Jason are you sure? I mean, I don't want to look stupid." Jason started to speak.

"Monica so about studying Friday..."

"Oooh... Jason, gotta go...sorry." I rushed off the phone and didn't even hear what he said. I just didn't have the energy to focus on Jason *and* Brian's dinner. By the time I finished dousing myself in my mom's perfume and flat ironing my hair, I did a twirl in the mirror. A purple velvet dress that came to the ankle with black stockings and black flats. I wore silver hoop earrings and wore just liner and lip gloss. My butt looked slightly large but hey you can't solve all problems in one day.

"Monica," My mom yelled. "Brian is here." My stomach did literal flips. I ran some more clear lip gloss across my lips and grabbed my black purse. I walked into the hallway and there was Brian in a black polo shirt and freaking jeans.

"Jeans, Brian? I thought you said business casual, what happened to that?" I huffed with my arms folded. "I am going to change."

"No, you can't, we'll be late, babe." I thought, *wow, he just called me babe and it always made me melt like butter.*

"Well, I don't wanna look crazy. It's the first time I can meet the rest of your family." He was right in front of me blocking me from my room.

"It's ok, the dinner will be at our house and you can grab something from Ashley."

"Yea, sure." Somehow Brian forgot I wasn't Ashley's size. She was about a 4 and I was a 14. I said nothing and went on to Brian's. Riding over there we passed the Winter Festival. It looked so whimsical and you could smell the street vendor food of fresh cinnamon on elephant ears to fried Oreos. I would rather be there than a t this dinner. But we were celebrating Brian going to Arizona on a full scholarship.?"::::::::::? I was a girlfriend now and had to play the part. At the dinner I walked in and everyone had on red t-shirts with jeans to acknowledge the Arizona colors. I felt like just slipping upstairs and calling my mom to come and get me. I saw Ashley talking to someone. I waved her over to me.

"Ashley, I could kill your brother telling me business casual." Brian came walking over with one of his cousins his age.

"Hey, Ash can you help my girl out with a change of clothes?" Brian's cousin turned his head to keep from laughing. I laughed along with his cousin although I was deeply offended. Brian was whisked away by some cousins.

"Ashley, how in the world does he think I can fit your clothes."

"Well, I have an old red t-shirt that you may be able to fit. Now the pants... I think my dad has some old shorts... I mean, I dunno." Ash was trying.

"It's ok, Ash, I will be fine." But I wasn't fine, I was mortified. Not only was Brian clueless to my size, but he didn't even tell me the dress was casual. At the party was Brian's parents, grandparents, aunts, uncles, and random cousins. Despite all of the clothing drama, Brian was showing me as the most beautiful thing in the world. Everyone he introduced me to he would tell them, "Hey, this is my girlfriend, Monica." It felt so amazing. When we all sat down for dinner, everyone was sharing fun stories of Brian and baseball and how much of a good person he had become. I was proud of him. He was becoming a great young man for just turning 17. But then every family has a few folks that are just a little bit extra. That would be Brian's Aunt Lori and Uncle Robert. According to Ashley, he used to play Major League Baseball back in the eighties. Although I found them annoying, Brian was leaning on his uncle's every word. Uncle Robert kept telling him about the dos and don'ts and how he was a baseball player back in the day. He sounded very narcissistic and controlling.

I whispered to Brian, "Hey, it's getting late, I can stay another 30 minutes."

"Oh, come on, babe, it will be ok, I really need you to stay." He looked at me with those pearly white teeth begging.

"It's ok, nephew, let her go, I mean y'all got school, right?" He said while taking a swig of a beer.

"You're right, Uncle Rob, come on, Mon. I can run you home right quick." I stood in the living room waiting for Brian to come back with Ash. She couldn't stop laughing about my outfit still. But she understood my feeling uncomfortable wearing other people's clothes and felt bad.

"Hey, Mon, sorry about earlier."

"It's cool Ash, I mean how would you know I didn't want to wear your dad's shorts?" We both started laughing. I decided to walk over to the kitchen to grab my mom a plate of chicken for later. Then Aunt Lori came into the kitchen.

"Monica, right?"

"Yes, ma'am, and you're Aunt Lori?"

"Yes, well look we only have a little chicken left, so don't take too much ok."

"Yes, ma'am" I put the 3 pieces for mom back in the tray. I went into the living room and sat on the couch thinking all I wanted was to get something for my mom. But I kept my feelings inside as it was Brian's night. I got tired of waiting so I went to look for Brian. He was out on the patio talking to his uncle.

"Boy, look, it's time you get serious, you are probably gonna go pro at some point and you're gonna need a serious girl or no girl." Brian sat quietly. "Brian, you have to think of your life as a business and who is gonna fit. This girl here tonight, I get its high school and you're having fun. But when you get into college you want to date somebody more baseball ready." My heart sank into my chest. But even more the fact that Brian didn't say anything made it worse. Although he was proud to be with me in public, it wouldn't be good enough for when he went pro. I don't know, it *was* just high school. I was about to turn 15 in a couple weeks, and he was leaving. It wasn't like I was thinking about marriage or anything jeez. I just couldn't shake that feeling that I was only good for certain reasons and couldn't be a forever girl. Even if I hadn't shaken the chubby off, I could be responsible, loving, and smart enough to be anyone's forever girl. Brian eventually found me and took me home. He was so excited about his dinner that I didn't bring up Uncle Robert's comment. The chubby in me just wanted to keep it to myself and accept the fact at least I had a boyfriend even if it was for a little while.

At school it was official, I was Brian's girlfriend. He picked me up for school every morning and walked me to all of my classes. It was his last semester of school, so he had an easy load. I also had new "friends" that wanted to sit next to me in class or sit with me at Miller's. But I took it all in stride as being with the most popular boy in town. Jess and I were going to class but stopped to chat.

"So how does it feel, superstar?" Jess was teasing me.

"I mean it's ok, it's like having a really good friend but with extra perks." Since Brian was such a hot commodity, we almost never had to pay anywhere we attended in Jeffersonville. We even went to the local town council meeting where Brian was being recognized for his athletic scholarship.

"Well Jess, let's hang later." Jess moved her hair off her eye.

"Why can't you meet after school?" I leaned against the wall.

"Girl, I gotta tutor silly Jason."

"Oh, ok cool. Well see you later girl." Jess looked puzzled but she let it go. I had put off his sessions for nearly 2 weeks because I was always with Brian doing something. So here I was back at the same table where WW3 almost erupted. "So, Mrs. Baseball how you been? I mean, I barely see you, girl."

"Everything is great, I mean Brian is really cool you know." I said proudly while turning some pages in my notebook.

"So, what are you doing for your birthday next week?" Jason changed the subject, apparently, he didn't like discussing Brian too much.

"I always do a dinner with my mom and the next day the girls and I have something planned." Jason pretended to be sad, tracking his fingers along his face to appear as if he was crying. "Ohhh...so, no big plans with the local celeb. I am so crushed for you." He grabbed his heart with his palm open. Jason could be such a smarty pants.

"He actually has some events with the baseball team because their season is about to start. So, I doubt he will be able to do anything for my birthday." I wanted to do something but I knew he would be busy even after he got home late Friday night. "Jason how do you feel about long-distance relationships?"

"In what way?" Jason was chewing his gum so loud.

"Look, gum smacker, do you not understand the term long

distance?" I said stretching out my neck.

"Well, Ms. Celeb, I don't think they work. But that's just me, you know." Jason didn't appear to be on the team of long distance. Jason pulled out a wooden brush and began to brush his fade. "My pops said my aunt and uncle did long distance and they got married but other couples never can do it. It's a hard commitment." He stopped brushing his hair and put it back in his book bag. I had forgotten that I wanted to apologize to Jason for Brian acting completely insane.

"Oh Jason, I just wanted to say again I'm sorry about Brian, you know." Jason looked up from his book a little angered.

"It's cool but I'm not gone kiss his..." He caught himself. "I can take care of myself, Mon, so let's just drop it." Jason got up and gave me a fist pound and left. Apparently, Jason still had no love for Brian and I just let it ride. I had a good time hanging with Jason and helping him with his schoolwork. He was turning out to be a good friend. I met up with the girls at my house on Saturday to go over my birthday plans. Jess was late as usual, but Shelly and Ash were right on time. I updated them on Brian and told them how happy I was to be in a relationship. But they didn't seem too impressed. No screaming, no tight hugs, maybe they were over Brian and me. Shelly interrupted to tell us about MTV playing the new Backstreet Boys song. We were so corny, but we loved Backstreet Boys. They had announced a contest to win tickets on their next World Tour. The rules where we had to make a video dancing to our favorite Backstreet Boys song. Since I had no video equipment, we decided to use Jess's and Philly would record it for us. Since lately he was obsessed with directing and had joined the film club at school. Every time we saw him, he was treating us like we were in some movie scene. Once he even wore one of those silly director hats. We clowned him for nearly a week. I said, "Ok girls I am gonna call Philly." All the girls were sitting on the floor with their legs crossed and holding hands like they were praying. Jess was actually singing to God. I told them all to shhh. The phone rang, and he answered almost immediately and placed him on speaker so they could hear. I laid it on thick. "What up, Philly my main man, my homie."

"Monica, what do you want? I was in the middle of shaving." The girls nearly spit out their snacks. Philly barely had any facial hair so what in the world was he shaving...

"Ok, Philly, look, are you interested in directing our video for MTV for us."

"MTV?" Philly asked like we were making something up.

"Yea, fool, MTV."

"Well, I have to think about a price." I looked at the phone with a frown.

"A price? What in the world are you charging for Philly? What videos have you done?" "Look I have to come up with a video plan and take time away from my studies, you know. The creative process ain't cheap, Monica." I decided to do a little psychological tactic with Philly.

"No Philly. it's not, so don't worry about it, I will ask someone else."

"Ok, I'll do it." He said it so quickly.

"Ok great, us girls decided Sat around 11 am works for everyone and you?"

"I mean that should work." Philly was hesitating.

"Look Philly in or out."

"Yes I'm in." I hung up the phone and told the girls we have a plan. After we decided on our outfits we had to come up with a song. The deadline was in 2 weeks, so we had to pick quickly. I wanted a slow song to really display our moves. Shelly wanted an upbeat song to dance to. We put it to a vote, and I won by pressuring Jess. We had to come up with choreography. Around 3 pm we decided to go to Miller's and order us a pizza. Jess was supposed to meet Mike afterwards to go bowling so we had to think quick. While eating I noticed some girls at the next table over just staring at me. Finally, one of them came over and started talking crazy. She was a short thick caramel girl with a French roll that needed to be re-done.

"Hey, we know you're with Brian and everything, but you just can't take people's seat." I looked at my girls like this chick is crazy.

"Um, look whatever your name is, this is our table." I stated staring her down.

"No, it's not, we were here first and went to the restroom." Miller's had open seating, so we hadn't noticed anyone sitting there when we walked in and sat.

"Hey, look it's no big deal ok, we can just switch tables." I waved for our crew to walk away.

"Yea, why don't you do that." I threw up my hands.

"Look y'all let's just go alright, apparently it's against the law to accidentally take someone's seat."

"What you say?" The girl looked at me seriously.

"Hey, I was just kidding alright so chill." She walked right up to my face.

"No, you chill." It started to get tense and people were looking.

After an intense staring session. I decided we didn't need the drama.

"It's cool y'all let's just go." Our crew started looking for another table.

"I don't know what Brian see in that fat cow, anyway." That was it, I had it with this short stop that looked like she just got off a land called delusional. She apparently thought she was dealing with a mouse, but she was about to deal with a BULL. Before I knew it, I gave my girls the nod to be ready. Her friends kept trying to calm her down, but she was ready to thump.

I walked straight into action, "Look you need to watch your mouth." The girl then looked around to make sure everyone was watching. "No, you need to watch what you put in yours. In fact, you shouldn't even be here eating. Isn't Jenny Craig waiting?" Before I knew it, I pushed the girl against the table. You could hear the table move. A crowd formed and she was trying to get off the floor. Her girls looked like they wanted to help but my crew was on standby if they tried to jump on me. My eyes were so lasered on her it could burn a hole through her face. Then I felt somebody grab me from behind and lift me away from the table. I was screaming "LET ME GO. I AM GONNA KICK HER BUTT." Whoever this was took me all the way to the back in the parking lot. But I was too busy trying to break away to notice who it was behind me. When I calmed down, I realized it was Brian and he looked furious. I was happy because I knew he really had my back and ready to go and check that stupid girl. He told me to stay here while he went inside. I was outside pacing back and forth, and he went back inside to settle the situation. Looking through the back door, Brian was able to calm everybody down. It was like he was some sort of diplomat... But then I saw him give the girl I was fighting a smile and they were talking. I banged on that window so hard I nearly broke it. Brian looked around to see where the noise was coming from. Then he saw me and put up his index finger in the girl's face. You would have thought that finger was worth a million dollars the way she was looking at it. He gestured for me to come inside. When I walked back in, I was already to finish the fight and my girls were ready too. But then I saw Mr. Miller and he looked heartbroken.

I said, "I am so sorry Mr. Miller, I will never do something like this EVER." The girls chimed in as well to apologize. Mr. Miller was always kind to us and gave us an outlet to hang and listen to all our favorite songs that our parents wouldn't dare allow us to hear. Mr. Miller was cool since the fight never took off but warned us it couldn't happen again. We all apologized again as we realized that Miller's just wasn't the place to do all of this crap. The crew went outside with me and the other girls stayed inside. We were all in the back area again talking about the situation. Brian came walking over to all of us extremely angry.

"What were you thinking Monica, and you too, Ash?" Brian was standing in between me and Ashley. "Y'all can't be out here FIGHTING." He had his hands on top of his head to where his hoodie rose and showed his stomach. The girls were all looking at me as if I had to speak up.

I backed up from Brian, "But Brian she was talking so much smack." He stared at me biting the inner of his jaw. Then grabbed me my belt hook to pull me closer. But I moved away and said, "No, you not right, Brian, I'm not going anywhere." I was hot and on 1,000.

Shelly spoke up, "Brian, look, it wasn't her fault, that girl started it." I felt like the fat girl that was always blamed for everything just because of my size. People always assumed it was the big girl, it couldn't be the smaller one. He tried to grab me again.

"Babe, come on, let's go" he said softly. I looked at him and I was now ugly crying. Every breath was quicker than the next one. Jess stepped in to calm me down. But Brian now stood behind me and placed his arms around me and made me walk to his car. Ash stepped in front of us and made eye contact with me. I told her in between breaths that I was ok. She told Brian to be cool and listen to my side. He was now calm and told her he would. While at his car, he still had me in a tight grip. I said in a low but serious tone.

"Brian, please let me go."

"Are you calm, Mon?" I didn't say anything, but he knew I was ok. It had turned a little cold and I didn't realize it because I was so fired up and all I wore was a hoodie. But I couldn't ask for his black peacoat. Because I didn't know if I could fit it. Brian got into his car.

"Hey, let's get out of here." Brian was calm, but still had an attitude.

"Where?"

"My house." Brian still was upset. I don't think it dawned on him that I would invite him inside since my mom would be at work. In reality, I just wanted to go somewhere with heat because I was freezing. Once we got to the house, Brian turned off his car and turned toward me. "Babe, listen." He said. I stopped him in mid-sentence.

"Brian, hold up, can we take this upstairs. Plus, I need to grab something for you to take to Ash."

"You mean you want to have this conversation with your mom

listening." He looked puzzled and his face scrunched up.

"She isn't home yet, she won't be back until late tonight." I had never done this, but I would rather risk my mother killing me than riding around freezing to death.

"You sure?" Searching my eyes for approval.

"Boy, I just want to talk, come on." While upstairs we sat in my living room. It's not that he didn't try to go into my room claiming that he wanted to see what it looked like. I told him it was messy and guided him in the front room. We jumped right to it as if we didn't miss a beat.

"Look, Monica, I need you to listen."

"No. You listen, Brian, do you even care?"

"Yes, I care, but you have to understand that you fighting can mess me up."

"How Brian? I ain't going to college." I was steaming mad and he knew it.

"Look I am leaving for college on a full ride, Monica. If them coaches think I'm hanging out with people that are fighting, I could lose everything. Also, if somebody mess with you then I'm gonna have to step in." I smiled a little bit on the inside.

"Whatever Brian, and then you gone laugh it up with that chick, thanks a lot." I said in a serious tone.

"Look Monica, I CAN'T HAVE IT." He slammed his hand on top of the wooden table.

"Ok, I GET IT...YOU DON'T HAVE TO SLAM THINGS." I yelled right back. I grabbed my coat and stormed to his car. He wasn't gonna yell and scream in my house. He ran out in the hall yelling my name. I got to the car and Brian leaned against the jeep with his head leaning back. I also had to lean back as well. After taking a couple of deep breaths. "Brian, I understand, and I don't want you to lose anything ok? This is all new for me." Brian gave me a side eye. It felt like Brian was taking me on a roller coaster. This turn here, and dropped off there. I knew being with him would be a ride, but I didn't expect this much drama so early. But he was it because I had no other transportation that was good. I took a long look at him and asked "Brian, I don't know if you realized, but you're my first boyfriend and I need you to be a little patient with me. That girl started things and I am nobody's sucka." Then I took a long deep breath. Brian's eyes still had hurt in them. "I will never put you in a position where you feel like I would betray you or hurt you."

"Babe, I know, ok, but remember we are now a couple and we have to work as a unit." I loved that he thought of us that way, but I knew he was leaving soon, and I didn't understand why he had so much faith in me. Brian was 17 and leaving to a whole other state where there would be all types of women. I hadn't even turned sixteen. He had a look in his eyes as if I were solid gold. I loved the way it felt even if it was only for a little while. He ended up taking me back to his house so the girls and I could finish the plan for the video and discuss the near royal rumble for the evening. On the way I got an earful of Relationship Rules 101 per Brian. Which meant constant communication and not embarrassing him in public. Since I was the "novice", I just listened.

Chapter 17

———◆—◆—◆———

The next week we met to talk about the video with Philly and all of these crazy ideas from riding horses to rapping in our pajamas. We decided to dress like the guys but with a feminine touch and call ourselves the Backstreet Girls. We had on baggy cargo pants with satin white shirts that tied in the front. Doing their exact choreography along with a little acapella at the end of the video of how much we loved their music. Jess and Shelly wrote the lyrics.

Tell me why
We love you so much
Tell me why
We all have a big crush
Tell me why
We never wanna hear you say
That we can't get in the concert that way.
It was so corny, but hey, so were we.

After rehearsal that day, I had Brian drop me off at Jess's house to record the video. But before we could record, they wanted to discuss my birthday. They figured since I had a boyfriend now my plans would change. I was bent on not changing my plans for anybody and became that cliché friend that leaves her friends for a guy. I mentioned, "Hey Ash did Brian say anything?"

"No, I don't think so, at least, not to me."

"Ok, well, y'all know all I like to do is watch corny movies and hang out."

Shelly chimed in, "How about *Dirty Dancing* and we wear our pjs?"

"Or we could have a mani/pedi night?" Ashley stated.

"Look guys I am ok with whatever as long as we get at least one corny movie and then whatever else is cool." It was Wednesday night and I had dinner with my mom on Friday and then the girl's night with the crew. Maybe I could hang out with Brian during the day on Saturday, if there was a possibility. I planned to mention it to Brian during the week.

My birthday finally arrived. I was turning 15. The dinner with my mom was set to be at 7 pm. I got dressed in a black pants suit. I rodded my hair into tight banana curls the night before to ensure it wasn't a wet mess like before. My mom left a note for me to meet her at the restaurant because she had an errand to run. My neighbor, Mrs. Goldblacks took me to the restaurant around 7:15 since momma would be late. I got there and the hostess said, "Oh you must be the birthday girl, everyone is waiting." I thought to myself, *everyone? She must have the wrong person.* I allowed her to walk me to the back of the restaurant and that's when I saw "everyone." My grandmother and family had driven from Alberta for my birthday. I was completely shocked. A million thoughts went through my mind as everybody started hugging me and saying, "Happy Birthday." Even my uncles drove down, and parties weren't there thing. I looked for my mother in between hugs and I spotted her talking to the waitress. We connected eyes and she gave me a big hug. I sat at the head of the table. The room had nice clean bronze walls with dark brown tables. It also had a shiny chandelier that hung over the long table. We all ordered our food and began small talk. I was so happy that my mom didn't have to go 3 rounds with grandmother over her career choices.

As I was eating an appetizer my grandmother asked rather loudly, "Sooo, where is this boyfriend of yours?" She said it as if she really didn't believe me.

I just politely answered, "I'm not sure…maybe he is with family." The whole table was staring at me with these silly smirks on their faces. This birthday was turning into a disappointment. It felt like everyone was here just to make fun of me. My mom said in a stern way, "Look, where Brian is at is nobody's business. I invited everyone here to celebrate Monica turning 15. And to open our lives up. Everyone at the table looked at each other stunned that mom had spoken up. For years mom only visited on Sundays and holidays. As she spoke, it felt like years of frustration was finally let out. "My child is great, yes I got pregnant and her father and I did what was best at the time, but we are doing just fine."

My grandmother interrupted clutching her pearl necklace, "Veronica! Please stop this outburst immediately."

"No, I'm sick of this crap, you come here and already making little jabs about Brian."

I intervened, "Mom, it's ok, I'm sure grandmother was just being polite." I wasn't being truthful at all, but I just wanted the drama to end.

"Grandmother, mom has worked really hard to put this party together and we normally just do her and I each year. So, it was big of her to invite everyone, so can we please just be nice?" Just when you could cut the tension with a knife my cousin Stephanie walked in bearing presents. She was an older cousin away at college and home apparently. Stephanie was my favorite cousin; she never made me feel bad about my size and would always tell me to gain confidence. She was tall just like me and built like a model. She had died her hair blonde to look like Faith Evans and had hazel eyes. I ran over to her so excited, literally tackling her. I spoke in her ear, "Please come and sit down. The fam is cutting up, man." Steph came and sat down and then the main food course arrived just in time. But I could tell my mom was still upset. I whispered to mom, "It's gonna be ok," She nodded her head back and forth, and just like that, we went back to our usual family gatherings. After we all had eaten, I went and sat next to my grandmother and asked, "So, grandmother, did you have an ok time? I mean, besides the obvious."

She replied, "Monica, I want you and your mother over Sunday for brunch."

I said slowly, "But uh… grandmother, I dunno, I mean, mom seems a little upset."

Then she gave me a long stare, "You let me worry about your mother, ok? And by the way Monica, Happy Birthday. Grandmother left you something special." I gave her a hug and she and some relatives left for Alberta. I knew my grandmother loved me, but I think secretly she believed my mom let me down by allowing me to get chubby. I told my grandmother I would do my best. Meanwhile, Stephanie and I sat and talked. I told her about my new friends and Brian, of course.

"So, how do you feel about Brian, really?" The question completely threw me off. I responded as honestly as I could.

"I mean I'm not really sure. I know I like him, and he really seems to care about me and…"

"Monica you're rambling."

"I know, but I can't help it. To be honest, Steph, I'm not sure how I feel about him yet. All I know is that he cares about me and I am learning how to be a girlfriend." Steph placed her arm on my shoulder.

"Monica, just don't give in to everything and remember to be yourself." As Steph prepared to leave, I went over to my mom and gave her a long hug.

My mom whispered softly, "Thank you, baby." When I got home, Mom and I started to open my cards and gifts. Although my family could be annoying, they sure gave some nice gifts. I asked my mom about inviting all the family.

"Mom why did you invite them?" She replied, "I just wanted to start fresh and well…I wanted my mom to see how well you were doing and my new job. I guess that blew up, huh?" We let off a chuckle.

"Oh, momma, one more thing?" She was walking out of my room.

"Yes, baby?"

"How come you didn't invite Brian?" She stopped and turned in the door.

"I did, but I guess something came up. It was short notice." I simply nodded my head and momma shut the door. I wondered why he didn't show up. Was he still mad? I guess I will find out later. Instead of pondering, I began to think about how to save my money for some trendier clothes. 1997 was here and so was fashion.

Chapter 18

Before getting ready for the evening with the girls, I went to the mall with my cousin Steph to get some fashion advice. I had gotten better, but I needed to get a whole lot better. I was someone's girlfriend and needed to keep up my part. While at the mall, we had a Cinnabon and lemonade. I never felt uncomfortable eating in front of Steph because she never judged me. I wanted to go to the Athletic Store to get some baseball jerseys. She told me I had all of this length and despite my chubbiness I had a great body. She talked about accentuating my features and not to be afraid to wear heels. So, with Brandy "Best Friend" playing in my head we found some knee-length skirts with little splits at the knee along with some fuzzy sweaters to match. Fitted shirts which I hated because my boobs were nowhere near flat. In fact, they would be considered rather large, so bad I wore two bras when cheering. We also gathered a couple of beanie hats to go along with the outfits. Steph knew me so well. I had the personality of a boss but the shape of a plumber. She asked, "Mon I will be leaving tomorrow afternoon for school. If you want, I can do your hair." I stopped in the middle of the mall like I had been electrocuted.

"What's wrong with my hair? Is it that bad?"

"Um, it's not bad, it's just the same curls, I mean thank goodness the braids are gone. Your obsession with Brandy is a bit much."

I crossed my arms, "Whatever."

She started to pull on my thick curls and said, "Ok you can wear these a couple times a month but no more braids." I pouted my bottom lip and Steph said, "We can do some twisties in the front and flat iron the back or rock a bouncy wrap. We will see, I have some hair magazines that we can look at."

We kept walking and then I yelled, "STEPH!!!" She looked like the building was on fire.

"What! Girl jeez."

"Steph my bad, I was just thinking you should stop by my girls only sleepover tonight."

"No, ma'am, I don't do teenage sleepovers."

"Oh, come on Stephanie, please my girls would love it."

"Nope...Nope... and heck no..." Smiling, "Ok I get it, I will see you Sunday."

I walked through the door all ready for my slumber jammy jam. My mom had a makeup center in the living room set up to give us facials along with a snack stand filled with different chips, sodas, and things to make an ice cream sundae. My mom also surprised everyone with satin pajamas like the ones from the TLC creep video. My pajamas were Ivory. Everyone else's pajamas were black. My mom always wanted me to stand out. I couldn't help but look at the size tags. I peeked into the girl's gift bags where they had makeup kits, pajamas and slippers. Ashley's were a size small as with the rest of the girls. I don't know why I constantly look to compare myself to my friends. I secretly wanted their sizes and the attention. My mom stopped and grabbed my shoulder, "Monica, you're smart, beautiful and you have a great boyfriend. Most girls would kill for that."

I shrugged my shoulders, "Mommy, I know it's just sometimes I just feel like I am just a tag along. You know, even with Brian I don't know. It's like he is with me because I am safe."

My mom was messing with the gift bags adding lip glosses and she looked up taking a deep breath appearing tired of my whining, "Monica what do you mean by safe?" I couldn't answer. I still couldn't believe he had chosen me to be his girlfriend out of all of the girls in Jeffersonville.

I just said, "Nothing mommy, just a thought I had. No biggie."

The girls arrived right on schedule with gifts on hand. I loved getting presents. It made me feel like people actually cared about me. First, everyone changed into their satin pajamas. Then momma and some of her old friends came by to do our faces. I was never skilled with makeup, but my mom's friends had my face glowing. I loved doing karaoke, so we decided to turn on the CD player and sing along to TLC's *Creep*. We pulled the lyrics from the CD case because I was a stickler at getting the words right. We sang:

So I creep yeah just keep it on the downlow.

Say nobody's else supposed to know.

So I creep yeah cuz she doesn't know what I do.

My mom glanced over giving me that stare of 'ok Monica the song is a bit much'.

I asked the girls if they were ready to watch chick flicks. Jess pulled me to sit down on the couch and said, "Well Mon we have a little surprise for you. Remember that video we did for MTV?"

I said with eyes looking from face to face, "Yea."

Jess sat next to me, "Well, it turns out we didn't win but one of the production staff went to college with my mom and she got us..."

I looked like a dog panting, "Got us what, Jess? Come on." Jess kept looking back and me then to the girls teasing us.

"We have 4 front row tickets to the Backstreet Boys summer tour with backstage passes." The girls and I screamed so loud my mom came running back in reminding us that we lived in an apartment. We all tackled Jess. It was so cool. All my doubts about being self-conscious flew away for a moment. We ate cake and ice cream. I didn't think for one second about my size, just having 3 great friends and family. My mom came in saying she forgot one of my gifts in the car from my cousin Steph. I was so excited I told her that I would go down and grab it. I threw on my coat so I wouldn't freeze to death. I walked swiftly to the car as the breeze was cutting through my pajamas like a knife. I ran back inside, and I heard someone whispering my name in the hallway. It's Jason standing there with a red puffy coat and a black beanie hat.

I whispered, "Jason" with cold puffs of air coming from my mouth. "What are you doing here?" He just stood there looking at me like I had stolen his money or something. "Jason, what's up? Why are you at my apartment?"

"Monica, we need to talk." I squinted my eyes at him like I needed bifocals.

"About?" I wanted to keep it short and sweet as my party was going on and I didn't want to be rude. Jason leaned against the wall with hands in his pocket and said, "Monica, I don't like you going out with Brian." I stood there in complete shock. I attempted to walk past him like what he said didn't matter. He rushed up behind me nearly pushing me into the wall. "Monica, please listen, it's just ever since we started being friends, I can't get you outta my mind. It's driving me freakin' crazy." I sat down on the beige steps in my apartment stairwell.

"Jason, I don't get you. First you kiss me and then you act like I don't exist and then play me for my homie. I can't see how you have these feelings."

"Look. I just came to tell you how I feel and give you your birthday present." Looking at him, I asked, "Jason what I am supposed to do, are you saying you ready to go public with me?" Jason looked down and had no words. I jolted up nearly slipping on my satin pajamas. "So that's it, huh? Jason you are something else." I slapped my thighs. "What's the freaking point?"

Jason was still against the wall, "I just wanted you to know my feelings." I stood up and looked at him pointing my finger on his forehead.

"Jason, the sad part is you don't see how every time you say you're not ready it's like driving a stake through my heart. For the record, I have a boyfriend that isn't afraid and friends that care for me. I don't need this friendship or to know you at all." Jason looked like he lost all color from his caramel face.

"Monica, please. I came over here to give you your present and then it hit me to be honest with you. I would think as friends you would like honesty." I started to walk up the stairs, but he jumped in front of me, grabbed my face, and just stared at me. He was looking at me so deeply that I couldn't take it.

"Jason I am done with this, leave me alone and lose my number." He didn't stop me that time. I got up the stairs and I told my mom I had trouble finding the gift and sat in the car to warm up. I didn't say anything to the girls about Jason showing up, it would start too much drama. The girls fell asleep around 2 am that night. I went to the restroom to open Jason's gift. It was a Backstreet Boys t-shirt with a note that said:

Happy b-day Monica,

I just need time.

I cried to myself as all the feelings I had let go of that night suddenly came rushing back.

My mom was yelling that Brian called and said he was on his way. I really didn't want to deal with any more drama, but I had to speak up. Brian came to pick me up at 11 am. I stood in my apartment hallway with a line of questions to fire at him once I got into the car. Always the gentleman, he opened the car door for me. The door couldn't even close before he started apologizing.

"Babe, I am so sorry about your birthday. I was with my uncle all weekend for a baseball thing with some alumni about me going pro. I am so sorry."

I said, "Brian they didn't have a phone at this event?"

"Look, Monica, I said I was sorry I don't know what else to do. Look I was planning on taking you out tonight but if you don't want to it's cool." I looked at him like I could have punched him in the mouth.

"Thanks Brian, I am good." I got out of the car and walked back upstairs. Brian just pulled off. I could hear his tires screeching. As I went to school Monday, I couldn't help but think that the 2 men in my life were being complete jerks and how I was better off being Big Mon with no date than this drama. The worst part is that I couldn't tell my girls about the Jason part. It all sucked. As my mom was driving me to school, I asked her "If you had something to tell a friend, but it may hurt them, would you tell them or keep it to yourself?"

My mom stopped in front of the school, "Monica always be honest even if it hurts." I thought about Jason being honest with me and how I reacted. So, what if he couldn't be seen with me, it was his truth. The result of that truth meant we couldn't be friends. It was then that I decided to inform Shelly and the crew about Jason even if it hurt.

Chapter 19

I got to my locker and Nikki was standing there with her crazy blonde hair. "What do yooou want Nikki?" I slammed my locker and walked down the hallway. Nikki was right on my heels like a dog. I got into the band room where no one was around. "Ok, Nikki, you have my attention."

"Heard you had a great birthday." I looked at her puzzled as to why she would care about my birthday.

"Yea, soooo…" Nikki then pulled out a chair and asked me to sit. While sitting she began walking around me like a police investigator rubbing her hands together slowly. I stood up and said, "Nikki I ain't got time for this crap so spill or I am out."

Nikki replied, "I told you I was gonna take you down, freshman. It's amazing what you hear in hallways. You know Marcia's cousin lives in your building and I so happen to be there Saturday night. I guess Brian isn't enough; you need your friend's man too."

My eyes got huge as marshmallows. "Nikki you must have me confused with your trifling ways. Yeah, I heard about you and Mike's little… situation. Don't come at me Nikki, like yo crap don't stink." Nikki pursing her lips together with that ugly bright red lipstick.

"Well, Ms. Monica, this ain't about me, and I already told everyone that you tried to steal Jason from Shelly. It's always the friend, huh?" I felt like I was going to puke. So, I did something I never do...I ran. I ran out of the band room searching for my girls so I could tell them my side. When I got to the cafeteria table, I knew that Shelly knew by the look on her face. I walked to the table slowly and sat down.

"Shelly I am sorry. I was going to tell you, but I didn't want to hurt you." Shelly and the girls ignored me as if I didn't exist. I looked up and the room felt as wide as the Red Sea. Jason on one side acting as if I don't exist and Brian with his groupies on the other. I felt like I did in middle school, alone and afraid. I felt like I was being pranked, and that they were only my friends out of pity or to win some bet. The silence was killing me, and I just had no words, so I left the table. I pretended to be sick and went to the nurse's office. My mom came and got me, but she had to return to work. I sat under my blanket and was planning on how I could transfer to another school. But then my phone rang. It was my cousin Steph. I was so happy to hear from her, I let out a big sigh of relief. Because Steph always had the answers. "Heard you had a rough day, cuz." I immediately burst into tears.

"I am a horrible person, Steph, I am not meant to have friends." Steph listened to me go on and on about Jason and how bad of a person I was yadda...yadda.

Steph told me, being the straightforward person she was, "Monica, you let your insecurities cost you. If you were more confident, you would have told your girls Jason kissed you. You never gave them the chance to be there for you because of your lack of confidence. How many times have you told them about your life? Let them know about your Dad or how Brian treats you like a child." I thought quietly about the one time I did.

"Steph, I told them about Brian, and no one cared."

"Monica, only once. You should have called them out. They can't be good friends if you don't allow them to be." It dawned on me that I had chubby issues, not them. Jason not wanting me was not their problem. I needed to tell them the truth. Finally, Steph said, ``Now shape up and be honest. It's never too late.''

Between sobs of tears, I told Steph, "Alright, cuz, I will."

I convinced my mom to let me stay home the next day as I had to process how I would apologize. I walked around in my big purple robe and sank back into my soaps. At least I could see other folks' lives messed up. The rest of the week I became invisible. I ate lunch in the library and rushed home after classes. I told Coach Minnie I was having personal problems, so she excused me for the week. While at home my mom walks in and tells me that I had a message on the machine. Beep.... Hey it's your Dad. Monica, your mom said we could all go to dinner sometime over your spring break but... well I will see you then. I looked over at my mom and she said, "Baby, it was time for me to be honest." Suddenly, I had a burst of energy and no fears. I was going to meet my Dad for the first time life was getting better.

After school Friday I went to Miller's. I knew the girls would be there scarfing pizza. It was like walking over to the cool kids table like the first time we met. My feet were like cement as I went over to the table. They were all sitting there in cheer uniforms looking just as sad as me. I asked, "Can I speak with you all?" They all looked at each other as if seeking approval, then nodded in unison but appeared hesitant. At that moment I lost all of my nerves and started to walk away. I got to the door and thought I am content with being alone, just me and my shows. And just like the first day of school Jess appears and asks me to come and sit back down. Her hair was even similar as the first day, she was rocking her signature flat ironed hair with her bangs over one eye.

Walking back to the table I sat down, and Jess said, "Look, Mon, we decided we should at least hear you out. I mean, we just assumed what Nikki said was true."

I got a little snappy, "Why? I mean dang, I get it sounded pretty bad and stuff, but I thought we were friends. You all don't understand how I felt." Ashley put down her red cup of ice looking calm. She had her hands folded while looking at me disappointed. Her pink hoodie covered her head so all I could see were her eyes piercing through.

"What about my brother? You were playing him. He took a risk to date you." As soon as the words left her mouth, she could tell it was a mistake.

"What do you mean by risk, Ashley?" Ashley placed her hand on her forehead and took a deep breath and lowered her voice.

"Monica, I meant getting serious with someone before college. You know how my family is with this college stuff. Come on, Mon, you know better." I unzipped my jacket to get more relaxed. I stretched my arms out to express myself.

"Y'all just don't get it. It was…" Shelly slammed her fist on the table angry at my comment. I looked over at her with my mouth open. I had never seen Shelly this angry.

"No, Mon, you don't know how I felt. You sat there and listened to me vent about Jason and even encouraged us to date. What is wrong with you? The whole time you were secretly trying to date him. We even had the friendship meeting. You could have told us. I just don't know if

I can even trust you."

I looked directly at Shelly, "Look, Shelly, I understand how you feel but Jason danced with me first at the football after party. I didn't think anything about it, but when I got to school he was asking you out on a date. He kept flirting. Then he cornered me in a classroom and kissed me." I had finally told the girls my secret and it felt good, but they didn't look too happy. "Look, whatever MAN!" I exploded. "Is that so hard to believe?" I was looking at them right in their eyes. "It's because I'm chubby, RIGHT?!!" People were starting to look over at us, but I didn't care. "I know you feel that way because I felt it too. That day I was so excited to have my first kiss…My first kiss, guys, and I was too ashamed to share it because I didn't want the stare that I see right now. How the very next day Jason was too ashamed to date me publicly." My lip started to quiver. "I felt so ashamed of something that was sooo exciting. Shelly, I am sorry for not telling you. It's just when he decided to date you instead of me it really hurt. Then when I saw you liked him I just… Shelly, I shut down." My face had become wet from tears. I started to rip up a napkin from nerves. "I have this thing of wanting to make my friends happy. You guys are gorgeous, and I thought if I said something I would lose you. I am sooo sorry for not saying anything, but I meant no harm." I looked around at the crew and there were tears streaming down their faces, but no words. They looked exhausted from dealing with my insecurities, but I understood this was my fault. They already told me how they felt about me before, but I just never believed them. I got up from the table and zipped up my coat. It was a snowy afternoon, but I walked home feeling relieved that I was honest and no matter what I would be ok. I still had issues, but it was a new beginning.

When I got home, I was too exhausted to even talk, so when I got to the door and saw my friends in my bedroom I was in complete shock. I unzipped my coat and ran over to the greatest group hug ever. The girls made me promise to always be honest especially about boys and to have confidence in myself. In this chubby season I shredded Big Mon, but I needed to work out my chubby problems. But looking forward to the spring I had my girls, my family, and a play to audition for at school. Things were looking bright; I went down to check the mail and I had 2 letters. Spring was gonna be interesting.

Epilogue

<hr />

Date: 1-30-97

Where: In class

Song: Use your Heart by SWV

Dear Monica,

I know what Nikki said about us. I know about the rumors. Look, my feelings haven't changed about you. I like you so much. I love your curves, your smile, and even your mind. You challenge me every day and you are so loyal. I know I hurt you by not wanting to go public but that was more to do with me than you. And after you started dating Brian, I just got jealous. I know you and Brian just broke up, so I heard. Philly told me to just go for it. So, shoot here it goes. Monica, I want to take you out on a date next Saturday. No strings, just dinner and a movie. I will meet you there at 7pm. If you show up great. If not, I will keep trying.

Love, ya boy Jason

P.S. use your heart

To: Monica

1-31-97

Hey babe,

I am so sorry for missing your birthday and just being a jerk. I had a lot of stuff going on with this baseball stuff. It's like everybody wants me to be this or that. But not you. When I first met you, I loved how you would call me out and be so trusting. I heard about the situation with Jason. I know you didn't kiss him, because I know you. But look, remember it's gonna be you in my life even after I go pro. I want you to be with me. 3 years isn't a long time and I decided to play in OH so we will be close. That's why I wasn't there for your birthday. I had it out with my family and decided to enjoy college before rushing to the pros after a year. I was just frustrated. I hope you can forgive me. Anyways I have a sports banquet in OH and I wanted to see if you were free next Saturday to go. My family will all be there. It's where I am gonna announce my college choice. Again, I'm sorry.

BRIAN

P.S. I got you a OH t-shirt no more awkwardness

Acknowledgements

---◆—◆—◆---

I would like to thank God who is the head of my life and whom without him I couldn't do anything. My husband you are amazing and my rock, leader, and love of my life. You helped me many nights listening to me develop this story over and over. To my daughter Olivia, thank you for inspiring me to write even on nights when mommy was tired. To my cousin Megan, thank you for dedicating the time to help me edit this book. It really helped. To my mom I love you and thank you for your continued love and support. Dad I love you for always pushing me to be great. Pops love you for all your support. Debbie thanks for your creative input. To my aunts and uncles I love you for always having my back. To my friends and church I love you all and thanks for the support.

Chubby Seasons is a fictional series about a young chubby girl coming into her womanhood in highschool. Girls who have curves almost always get overlooked in life. I wanted to showcase a curvy girl through adolescent years that gains popularity but still has to deal with "chubby girl issues". Jeffersonville is a fictional town of upper class African Americans. It is important for me to showcase that side of our culture that can sometimes get overlooked. The book is based in the 90s because it's the time I grew up and I love the music created during that era. The next season we will see how Monica adjusts to the second half of her freshman year. With the upcoming school play, her friendships, and whether she chooses Jason or Brian will be a definite jaw dropper. I want to thank you for reading and I hope you enjoy the first of many books in the Chubby Season series.

For updates on my book please follow me on Facebook @Chubby Seasons page or email me at chubbyseasons@gmail.com for more updates.

Made in the USA
Monee, IL
18 April 2021